A CASTLE FOR

THE KOPCHEKS

A Castle for the Kopcheks

by

JAMES STAGG

The Macmillan Company
New York

First American Edition
First Printing
English edition published by
Ernest Benn Limited, 1963

Library of Congress catalog card number:
64-15458
Printed in the United States of America

FOR HELEN AND PETER

From quiet homes and first beginning,
Out to the undiscovered ends,
There's nothing worth the wear of winning,
But laughter and the love of friends.

HILAIRE BELLOC

CHAPTER ONE

How WE got to England is a story in itself, and one day I may tell it. But just now that isn't the story I want to tell—maybe I want to forget about that part of our life anyway. They say that with a strong enough reason you can make your mind do what you want, so perhaps there will come a day when I can forget it. The story I want to tell is what happened when we got to England. It's a story that nearly ended in tragedy for us; though, I see now, we were in part to blame as well as the others.

Our name is Kopchek, and we consist of Mama, Bradislav, Sandor, and me—Sondra. We came from an eastern European country, which I won't name, because I want to forget that too. Our father is dead, and, because of what he was and what he did, we love his memory dearly.

Bradislav is thirteen, two years younger than I, sturdy, with dark, crisp hair like Father's and a squarish face with a determined jaw. Brad is quick to rouse and is intensely loyal. He has a taste for happiness and by nature is gay; though, to tell the truth, in the past there has not been much opportunity for that. Sandor is nine, tow-haired, and has bright-blue eyes. He has an upturned nose and a serious face. He smiles rarely, but when he does it's as if someone pulled the curtains in a dark room. Sandor has one leg longer than the other and walks with a limp. We try to ignore it as much as Sandor so fiercely ignores that handicap. But there are times when his leg so completely defeats him that we cannot fail to notice it, and then there is a quiet sadness in all of us for a while.

And Mama—what can I say about her that will paint for you the wonderful picture of what she is? For a little while I will try to pretend that I don't belong to her, though I even have her name; that I'm outside the family and will therefore be less likely to overpraise her. Mama is a little over medium height for a woman, and she has corn-colored hair about which she is not too pleased and which she calls—now that she has seen cottages with roofs of straw—her thatched roof. She has a wide forehead across which there are thin lines, though you have to look close to see them. Frankly, I love them, for they are visible proof of the worry and care she has had in her heart for all of us. They are the signs of her love for us, and in the past we have had only that love to cling to. Beneath that broad forehead her large brown eyes sparkle. Sometimes—only very briefly, however—there is a faraway hint of sadness behind the sparkle. And then I guess that some little thing has happened to cause her to remember Father in a special sort of way. Mama's nose is perhaps just a little too big, but her eyes and the soft, beautiful lines of her mouth prevent you from noticing her nose. She has a rounded chin with just the suspicion of a dimple, which she says was put there to remind her that she is inclined to be vain and to act as a gentle curb on her vanity. She is gentle and kind, but she also has a deep-rooted drive and quiet determination. If she hadn't, we should never have arrived in England. At the time we came to England, Mama was thirty-five and lovely.

Father we had left behind in a grave in our old country, where he had been killed fighting for what he believed in. I can remember him smiling at our questions as to why there was trouble in our country and saying, "It's because of a lot of things, sweethearts, but mostly because some people forget there are such things as compassion and dignity in a human being. Long words, eh? But one day you'll know them and will understand what I mean and all the things those words mean." I think, in our way, we understood what he meant, even then.

We got to England after what seemed like nightmarish adventures, and finally we arrived at Chadhaven. Mama took us there because Father, who had been a writer, had visited England many years before and had stayed for a few days at Chadhaven, which he loved and often spoke about in later years. Father had taught us all English—a language which was forbidden at our schools. "Apart from it being the language of a people who, for all their faults, have a reasonable sense of what is right and what is wrong," he told us, "it is the language of poets."

Father loved poetry. We didn't, but we didn't mind learning English, and we used to have one English-speaking day each week when, at home, we all spoke in English, with small penalties for lapsing into our native tongue. Father had made friends with some of the people at the British Embassy, and we had long talks with them when they visited us. That is, until the trouble began and we couldn't see them any more. However, those talks with English people in our old country enabled us to hear the language as it was spoken by its people, and that helped us a great deal.

Imperfect and quaint though it was at the time of our arrival in the new country, our English stood us in good stead and, in the beginning, made things easier for us. We had a feeling of relief and happiness at being in England, which Mama had decided should be our new home and in time our country. But that was before we went to Chadhaven and before we met the Cranstones, who were to have such an influence on our lives. I often think: What *would* have been our story if the Cranstones hadn't come into our lives?

•

As soon as I saw Chadhaven, I understood why Father had loved it so after only a few days there. In the days when the Vikings rowed up the creeks and river mouths of England, Chadhaven had been a thriving village. It stood at the edge of flat but solid land at the mouth of the River Chad, which emptied itself into one of a series of creeks that veined a wide stretch of marshland. A mile inland rose steep, wooded hills, which in one place had been gashed as if by a giant's ax. This was the path to the sea cut by the Chad, which in turn was fed by a number of small streams draining the hills. There had been a time when oak trees from the timbered hills were felled for the great wooden ships that were built at Chadhaven; but the Chad had protected itself from the onward march of time by carrying mud to silt up some of the creeks and extend the marshland, so that now Chadhaven was further from the sea than it had been in the Vikings' days, and had escaped the ugliness of industry.

It was old and proud of its age, and it sat at the edge of the marshland under the shelter of its hills; its people made small sailing craft to skim along the creeks under bright red sails and constructed sleek yachts that cut graceful lines in seagoing races.

The marshes, humped frequently with small dry-land patches, were covered with tall reeds and were the homes of countless water birds and wild fowl. Attempts throughout the years to keep the marshes from becoming completely covered by water had resulted in an intricate system of ditching and dikes, the full extent of which few people knew. The hodgepodge drainage system worked, however, and the marshes remained an area of beauty and the source of life for many wild things.

From the two quarries in the hills came the beautiful yellowish-gray stone with which most of the buildings in Chadhaven were constructed, and from the marshes were cut the reeds with which many of the houses and cottages were thatched.

There was an air of quietness and ease about the small town, so different from the tensions we had always known. It was easy to see why Father had loved this place.

During the time we had been in London, Mama had been a dynamo of energy, leaving us in the hostel where we were staying for entire days sometimes. This was necessary while she saw this person and that and proved her identity as Sondra Kopchek, widow of Miklosh Kopchek, the author, to whose credit in a London bank stood an amount of money which was the accumulation of royalties on two or three of his books which had been published in England. All that took some weeks—weeks of inactivity for Brad, Sandor, and me but of hard work and a great deal of travel for Mama. And so when we arrived in Chadhaven, having journeyed by train to Minthampton, the big seaport some twenty miles along the coast, and changed to the local line for Chadhaven, all was arranged. Or nearly all.

With Father's money, Mama had bought a house—and that was the thing that set in motion all the difficulties that dogged us. But the time for telling about that is not just yet. With most of the small amount left, Mama, who had already paid two visits to Chadhaven while we were in London, had bought a little furniture, just enough to make the house habitable. A few pieces of the most necessary household furniture was all she could afford.

Earlier, in London, when she first told us her plans, I had asked, having had plenty of time to think in the loneliness that only a city like London can breed, "But how will we live, Mama?"

Mama gave a smile of happiness. "I shall work, my sweetheart. Work at anything for any length of time. There is what they call a grammar school at Chadhaven. It is not what they call a state school, but it has departments for boys and girls, and the people here who know about it say it is a wonderful school. And when you first and then Brad and then Sandor have become good scholars in the English way, with good jobs, then maybe I will retire, and *you* can work for me, eh?"

"That's what we'll do, Mama," said Brad, full of enthusiasm. "Father hoped I would be a doctor. Maybe I can still become one."

"Of course you will," Mama had answered gaily. "So big a doctor you should become, maybe you'll be a doctor to the English royal household and wear a crust."

"Crest, Mama," I corrected her.

"Crest, crust—what does it matter? Brad will get it whatever it is." Mama had faith in us too.

When we—who had lived in nothing but a small flat in our old country because Father was not in favor with the government there—asked Mama what the house was like, she just smiled again and said, "Wait and see. It's a palace."

We knew Mama. She was given to exaggerating a little. She has looked out of our flat window in the old country at some aircraft flying over. "Oh, Miklosh," she has said to Father, "there are thousands of planes up there."

And I can remember Father looking up at her from his reading with no smile on his face, but loud laughter in his eyes, to ask seriously, "*How* many, Sondra?"

Mama, still looking up at the sky, would answer, "Well—dozens, anyway."

"Sondra, sweetheart—how *many?*"

Mama would turn, smiling at him from the window. "There I go again, don't I? There were four."

So when she said the house was a palace—well, we smiled with her. For truly, any house where Mama was would have been a palace to us. But in regard to the house, she gave us the surprise of our lives.

I wasn't sorry to be leaving London. It had been vastly interesting, and in some ways it had thrilled us. While Mama was working to build our lives anew, we had been shown all the wonderful sights of this historic, sprawling city. It was a deep emotional experience for Brad and me to see the Mother of Parliaments and to sit in the Strangers' Gallery and listen to a debate in the House of Commons. For this way of life had been what Father believed in with such fervor. It was what he had died for. It was what he had taught us to believe in, and we had suffered for it.

I don't know what we expected when we arrived in London. Somehow I thought that all these people ought to know what we had suffered because of the belief we had in their way of life and that somehow they ought to acclaim us. But they didn't, of course. They ignored us, and I, most unreasonably, felt a resentment growing inside me against this vast, unheeding, seething London, in which there were so many people and so much loneliness. So it was good to be going to Chadhaven.

We were bundles of eagerness, with our old suitcases and boxes and parcels, as we burst out of the small train at the station at what I later learned was called the Top End of the town. And we stood there looking around at the new sights to add to those we had collected during the train journey.

It was an early March day, and the residue of winter still hung about the crisp air. After London, there was a clean, fresh smell about the place—and more brightness and color too.

Mama said, "And so! Now we walk."

We had agreed, now that we were in what we hoped would become our new land, to speak nothing but English, and in those early days we often translated our own idioms into English—with mixed success. Brad and

I spoke the new language quite well already, though our pronunciation of some words would have puzzled the natives.

Brad picked up the two battered suitcases—the handles of which had been reinforced with string—and Mama distributed the rest of the boxes and parcels between Sandor, me, and herself. We had, of course, been able to bring nothing from our old country except a few clothes and a few things of Father's for love's sake, so that pretty nearly everything we possessed we stood up in. There had been no money left to buy new suitcases to carry our small supply of clothes. After the money Mama had spent on the house and furniture, there was only a very small balance left over, and this had to be kept for food and such things until Mama had found a job. About our old cardboard suitcases, Mama had said, "So why should we buy new? Our traveling days are over." I felt a tinge of shame at our shabby traveling containers, when I should have been proud of them—proud of them as being the badges of Mama's courage in refusing to accept a way of life she believed with all her heart to be wrong. At great danger to herself, she had uprooted us so that we could grow up in a true freedom of spirit and thought.

We set off, Mama and myself in front, with Brad and Sandor coming along behind. It was late afternoon as we started down the gentle slope of the main road leading into the old part of the town, and the March sun, still gathering the strength it would need for the days of spring and summer, was well down to the west. The gold with which it splashed everything was pale, but the lovely stone buildings of the town took hold of it and then threw it back to brighten the streets.

Ahead of us we could see the town proper as it stood in two parts on either side of the Chad, which had broadened into an estuary. And we could see the wide creek beyond and the lighthouse at the mouth. The houses we were passing were new, built in the lovely colored stone quarried from the hills behind us. Some of them had tiled roofs, while others had brand-new thatch. The houses in the old part of the town were mellow and the thatch mature, and near the mouth of the river, before it broadened out into the marsh-lined creek, stood the ruins of a castle.

"How far have we to walk, Mama?" I asked.

She turned to smile at Sandor, who was limping along easily for the moment. "Not far enough to tire Sandor," she said so that only I could hear.

"How far, Mama?" called Sandor, who had heard only my question.

"Just a short way, darling," answered Mama over her shoulder.

"Phew!" breathed Brad in mock exhaustion. "It had better be a palace when we arrive."

"You'll see," said Mama happily.

At the mouth of the river and in the creek, the masts of sailing boats made a matchstick forest. It seemed that everyone in Chadhaven must own a sailing boat.

The road ran by the side of the river all the way into the old part of the town, and the river flowed briskly. We passed a flour mill on its banks, and where the water poured into the dam there was a continual roar as it surged through, making the electricity which ran the machinery of the mill.

People we passed looked at us. They didn't stop and stare, but when we had gone by I could feel them turn and watch us. And I got angry with myself because it was then I became most ashamed of our shabby clothes and suitcases and parcels. I felt my face burning, and Mama saw it. She smiled at me. "We should have a goat with us," she said, "to make it really worth their while looking at us."

"Why a goat," said Brad, "when you've got me, who feels like a donkey, carrying this weight?" Brad was grinning, and Sandor giggled, but I couldn't even smile.

We walked right through the old town, through its narrow Fore Street, which still had cobbles at the side. We passed the church—square, solid, immeasurably old, and guarded by a squat tower. Now we were on a sort of grass-grown quayside, a lovely open space, with one or two elm trees, still leafless and brown, lacing up into the sky and crowned with rooks' nests. At one side, close by the wall built up from the river, was a narrow road leading right to the point of land at the mouth of the Chad. Here the road ended where the firm land met the marsh.

Near this point were two large houses standing separately in their own big gardens. Unlike most of the houses in the old part of the town, they were roofed with thick slates of the same color as the lovely yellowish-gray stone with which they were built.

Brad said, "Either we are going to live in a boat or in some secret building amongst all those reeds in the marsh or we're going to live in one of those two houses."

Sandor looked around. "There's nothing else," he agreed.

On the other side of the river, right opposite us, were boatbuilding yards, from where the sounds of the craftsmen at work came.

I looked at Mama. She was trying not to burst with excitement and not to talk or anything just yet.

We were level with the first of the two houses, bordered by a low, mellow wall with a higher hedge growing behind it, when the string on one of my parcels slipped. I stopped and placed the other on the ground to retie the one that threatened to spill its contents. Mama and the boys walked on. They were some twenty yards ahead by the time I had retied the parcel and was about to get up from my stooping position. Suddenly from quite close I heard a voice say, "Great Scot! There go our crummy refugee neighbors. Just look at them. What a shower!"

For a brief second I wanted the ground to open up and swallow me because of the shame I felt. And then I saw the thread-worn backs of Mama and Brad and little Sandor, full of hope, with their parcels and old suitcases, walking toward the future. I remembered all they had gone through. I remembered the struggle and the danger—and Father.

Suddenly I was blazingly angry. I sprang up and took two or three steps forward to where a gate stood open leading to the house. A boy, a little older than myself, stood just inside the gate. With him was a girl about my age. It was the boy who had spoken.

I went to him, one parcel under my left arm, the other held in my left hand by the string. My right hand was free. I swung it hard, palm open, my hand flat, and hit the boy on the side of his face so hard that the slap of it echoed across the river.

Into his startled face I shouted, "I hate you! I hate all the English!"

Then with hot, scalding tears streaming from my eyes and onto my burning cheeks, I ran after Mama and my brothers.

CHAPTER TWO

Mama and the boys had already turned into the gateway of the second house, which stood in a large garden reaching to the edge of the marshland. When I turned into it, still sobbing, they were standing there waiting for me. Mama had her arm very firmly round Brad's shoulders. He had put the battered suitcases on the ground, and his face wore a fierce, sullen, dogged expression—if one face can carry all those feelings at the same time. And Brad's could. Mama's face was set, and Sandor was looking a little bewildered.

"Mama," I said, "I'm not going to like it here in this place. I . . ."

"Hush, sweetheart," said Mama softly. "We heard what that boy said—his voice is loud. And we heard what you did and said. Your slap was even louder. I had to stop Brad from running back and hitting him again. This is not right. We shall ignore the boy and what he said. Remember—the hound that bays loudest is often furthest from the quarry." Mama had an unending store of sayings and axioms, many of which, I now suspect, she made up on the spur of the moment. Generally, however, they helped her make her point with us, though sometimes they appeared to have no bearing on what was happening. Then we would all laugh quietly together, including Mama.

"We are going to like it here," Mama went on. "This is going to be our home. People will like us because we shall show them that we want to like them. Don't forget we are strangers—and we may be strange to the people who live here, just as they are strange to us. But slowly we shall know each other and maybe like each other. And one day, if it is so willed, we shall become British." She raised her hand and smiled at me as I drew breath to say that I never would do that. "No—don't say it, Sondra, my named one. Look—let us look at ourselves. We maybe do look funny—odd—like this, eh? Soon it will be different. Come—if we look funny, let *us* laugh at ourselves and enjoy the joke too. Now—into our home with us. It is wonderful, but there is much to do."

My face was still wet with tears and stiff from the tension of crying, but I could see, even from where I stood, that there was indeed much to do. For one thing, it seemed most of the paint had been weathered away from the woodwork. That was the first thing that struck me. The second was the size of the house. Mainly it was two-storied, but there were also two gables facing out toward the marshes and the sea beyond, and there were rooms in these under the eaves. It was much too big for us—even if we took two bedrooms each.

Mama's gaiety was infectious. Brad's scowl disappeared, and Sandor's puzzled, worried expression was chased away by one of his day-brightening smiles as we followed Mama to the front entrance of the house—double doors, standing in an attractive rough-hewn stone porchway. Only I, it seemed, still felt an angry bitterness at having heard the remark made by the English boy. At that time, we were very poorly off for English idioms, and I had not understood what the word "shower" meant, but it had been the contempt and derision in the boy's voice which had cut so deeply.

Mama flourished the key. "We maybe ought to have a bottle of champagne to break, like they do when they name ships and launch them," she said as she put the key in the lock.

"But the house has got a name already," said Sandor, pointing to a wooden name plate fixed to the wall of the porch. The words could just be made out. "Look—'Light View.' "

"Ah, so!" said Mama, leaning to look at it as if she were seeing it for the first time. " 'Light View'—it's a nice name, a happy name. First thing, we shall paint it again. Now—here it is." She flung open one of the double doors and reached across the porch to turn the handle of the inside door, which she opened too. She was like a conjurer producing his best trick.

The boys, smiling and bowing with exaggerated

flourishes, motioned me in first. They followed, and Mama, her pretty face beaming, came in last.

I stood there, in the bare hall, wanting to cry again. It was so dingy and forlorn. Mama said, "This is the hall. One day we will have nice furniture. Now, in here is where we shall live and eat for the time being." She opened one of the doors leading from the hall, and we followed her into the room. It was a sizable room with big, bare French windows opening onto the large garden that swept, in a stretch of overgrown grass, down to a low stone wall at the edge of the marsh.

The floor boards had no covering and were dirty. In the room stood a bare deal table and four secondhand wooden chairs. That was all the furniture there. Old and ugly wallpaper peeled from the walls, and some of the winter's cold still clung to the room.

Mama took us through the house, talking happily all the time. The kitchen had an old gas stove, an old cupboard, and a small table. There was a sink and a drainboard. There were other rooms on the ground floor—maybe a dining room and two sitting rooms. They were completely empty and in the same state as the one we were to live in.

Upstairs, beyond the broad staircase that climbed gracefully from the hall, were eight bedrooms and a bathroom. We each had a bedroom, the boys' rooms having a single bed and a box by the head of them to act as a bedside table. Again, the floors were bare and the wallpaper faded. My room was similarly furnished, except that I had a small wardrobe and curtains at the window.

"This," said Mama crisply, "is how we start. Upstairs are two more rooms, and there, because there are things off the roof, the rain has come in and made it damp. Tomorrow we see about your schools, and then I start to clean the place. When it is scrubbed clean, then I find work, and slowly we will make a home."

It was twilight now, and Sandor turned on the electric switch. The light came on, shining harshly out of a naked bulb suspended from the ceiling.

His face lit up. "Mama—it works," he said.

Mama smiled. "Of course it works, darling. When I came to see the place I had to arrange for the electric light, the water, and the gas to be all turned on again. The house has been empty for a long time."

"And there are windows broken," I said miserably.

"Yes," Mama said, "there are windows broken, but they will mend easily."

"Don't look so miserable, Sondra," said Brad. "Mama has worked hard to get this home for us. We can put things right. Look at the house next to us—pretty garden, shining paint—a bright, happy place. We will make this a happy house also."

"They've got curtains at all the windows too," said Sandor. "It does look a happy place."

I couldn't look at any of them. "Nothing will make *this*—this *ruin*—a happy place," I said bitterly. I went out of the room and downstairs to the room in which we were to live and eat. This, I told myself, was worse than the conditions under which we had been living in the old country. I looked out of the French windows, which were bare and stark. Over the marshes an evening mist powdered the reeds, and the sky to the west still had a tinge of red gold low down. The room behind me was gloomy in the twilight. I told myself that this dreadful feeling I had in my heart was not shame—I had driven that from me when I slapped the boy's face. At the back of my mind I knew that, no matter what, I should have been full of pride and love for Mama, but at that moment I felt that by coming here to this ruin of a house, she had let us down. It didn't occur to me then that we were far more fortunate than most refugees in a foreign land. There had been some money we had been able to use. But why, oh why, hadn't Mama put it to better use than buying this ruin of a house?

There was a sound behind me, and I turned to see Brad come into the room with an armful of wood and logs. He looked at me without smiling and dumped his load on the hearth. He said, "I don't understand you, Sondra."

"You're not qualified to, anyway," I answered pettishly.

As Brad left the room, Sandor came in carrying a tablecloth and some knives and forks. He started to lay the table, and I turned back to the window to look out at the darkening sky.

There was a rustle of linen as he spread the cloth and

the sound of the knives and forks being laid on the table. Then I felt his small hand take hold of mine.

"Don't worry, Sondra," said Sandor. "We have Mama, and that's a good thing. And we're all together." Then he turned and limped away, and from the kitchen came the smell of cooking.

Little Sandor had hoped to comfort me; instead, the touch of his small hand and the words he had spoken brought tears to my eyes. Now I know that they were tears of self-pity and that I should have forced them back angrily, gone to the kitchen, hugged Mama, and helped with the cooking. But I didn't. I wallowed in my self-pity and let the tears run down my cheeks. Suddenly I didn't want to grow up. I wanted to be a little girl again—younger than Sandor—so that I wouldn't understand any of the things that were happening, nor be expected to. And I could run to Mama and bury my head in her lap and weep. And she would hold me in her motherly softness, and the love that always surged from her would warm away whatever coldness and harshness was hurting me. Then in her love and strength my tears would disappear.

But at fifteen I couldn't do that. I was nearly an adult. I was the eldest, and Brad and Sandor should have been able to lean on me as well as on Mama. I heard their voices in the kitchen. The meal seemed nearly ready. I couldn't face food or my family just then. I turned and ran up the bare, hollow-sounding stairs to the room I was to sleep in.

I lay on the small bed staring blankly into the darkening room. It was cold, so I pulled a blanket over me. I lay in the dark in shame and misery and with a dislike of everything English. After a while I got up, undressed, and went back to bed.

It was quite dark and a full moon was hanging low in the sky when the door opened and Brad came in.

"Sondra—you're not asleep?" he said.

"No."

"Good. Because I want to talk to you."

"I don't want to talk."

"There's no need for you to talk. I'll talk, and you'll listen." He came further into the room, and there was a coldness in his voice. He sat on the bed at the foot. "I can't understand what is the matter with you, Sondra," he said after a few moments. "All the time we were on our way here—all that horrible time—you were wonderful. Now when we have succeeded in doing what Mama set out to do—to be able to build a new life in a new country—you suddenly become different. We have all been through hard times, and it has been especially difficult for Mama. And yet she has done all this—for us—so that we shan't know the tragedy she has lived with for so many years."

"We shared it with her. And we loved Father too," I said, the side of my face pressed into the pillow.

"Yes, but close as we were to Father, Mama was that much closer. It was different, I think . . . a different, deeper depth between them."

Brad's words, and the long thinking that must have gone before them, surprised me. It showed a sympathy and understanding I never suspected him to have.

"Your words, and the way you have acted, have hurt Mama more than you will ever know, more than I will ever know. Oh, like Mama, she made excuses for you. But I have no excuses for you, Sondra. It is a wonderful thing Mama has done. And we, Sandor and I, are going to work to make this house beautiful for her, to try and show her how wonderful we think she is."

He stood up, and I could feel his brown eyes—Mama's eyes—looking at me.

"You're wrong about nearly everything, Sondra," he went on. "What did you expect when we came here? That the Queen of England should give us all medals? That the people should stand in the streets and cheer us?"

But I remembered that boy. "They are so smug and self-satisfied and self-centered—and that boy . . ." I said.

"Ah," said Brad, "there I agree with you. He had no right to be so insolent, and only Mama stopped me from adding a punch to your slap. I don't know why it is so, but most people won't welcome us. I heard Mr. Krawiczk—the man who runs the hostel in London—tell Mama that they accept us refugees here as a sort of burden. Like a duty. A lot of them think that their money will have to be spent to keep us. Well, Mama means to show them that with us, anyway, it is not so.

We will work and build our home and be a burden to no one. I'm sorry, but I'm not very pleased at the moment to have you as my sister. Tonight you have hurt Mama so much."

I heard his footsteps cross the room, and I heard the door shut softly.

Brad's words and the tone of his voice burnt into my brain, and I could feel an anger welling inside of me—anger against myself because I had not the depth of understanding my younger brother had. That *he* should lecture *me*. I wasn't angry with Brad, though.

What he said was true. If only that horrid creature of a boy hadn't said what he did—or, at least, if I hadn't heard him just then, at that time—I could have weathered the shock of the tumble-down house and the bareness of it. My thoughts dived away from me at a tangent.

Bare? How could it be bare with Mama in it? How could I have been filled with such self-pity, after all that she had gone through? Suddenly I remembered that Mama hadn't shown us her room when she had been taking us round the house.

I flung the bedclothes from me and got out of bed. I put a coat over my pajamas. Then I went out onto the landing and found Mama's room, into which the moon was shining. I knew as soon as I entered why she hadn't shown it to us.

Mama had no bed—she had no mattress. She was sleeping on a blanket on the bare boards. Nearby, there was a wooden box over which her clothes were neatly folded. And now the tears that were again in my eyes were not for me. I must have made a sound, for Mama sat up.

"Sondra?"

I was standing in the shadows, and at the sound of her voice I ran forward and dropped to the floor beside her, my arms around her, my face buried in her breast. And then her arms were around me, and a castle of defense against all my misery had suddenly sprung up. For a long while she held me as my tears spent themselves. At last I said, "I'm sorry, Mama, for everything."

"Hush, darling," she answered. "I should have told you it wasn't a palace we were coming to but a house that needed love and care to make it better. Instead, I was exaggerating again."

"But, Mama, couldn't we have had a flat in London—or here, even—and not spent so much money to *buy* a house?"

Mama hugged me more tightly. "No. With the money, we had the chance to put down roots—real roots—so that we could feel a part of the land, the country, and the people we have come to. Don't you see that, Sondra? What have we had before?"

"But all that money—and no furniture, clothes . . ."

"Work—I'll work at anything, and we will get the money for these things."

"But you can't do that—all on your own."

"I can—if I know I am putting roots down for my

children. You and Brad must work too—at school—so that when the time comes for you, too, to earn your living in the outside world, you can work in good positions and live a comfortable life."

Mama pushed me away from her a little to look at my face in the moonlight. "As for that boy"—she smiled—"my lovely redheaded firebrand—you dealt with him." Her face became serious again. "It was not right for you to have done that, but . . . One of these days, you'll be *proud* to apologize. Not now. But one day, when we have done all that we are wanting to do—when our house is mended and happy and we really *belong* to our new country—then there will be no shame in apologizing. Do you see what I mean?"

I didn't. *He* would have to apologize first before I spoke such words. So much of what I felt couldn't be wiped out just like that. Mama saw the look on my face and understood. She smiled at me again and hugged me. "One day, be sure, you *will* see what I mean. For now, we have many plans to make, so much to do. And —most important of all—we are *free* to do it. Tomorrow we start!"

Some of Mama's burning faith transferred itself to me. Some—not much. But enough to make me feel happier. I hugged her, and we stayed silent for some time.

"Mama," I said at last. "Now I feel hungry. I'm going down to the kitchen to get something to eat."

"I'll come too," said Mama. "I couldn't eat at supper-time, and I'm hungry as well."

We went down into the kitchen and began frying sausages.

Five minutes later the kitchen door opened stealthily and Brad crept in, tensed, a thick piece of wood in his hand. He relaxed when he saw us and gave us a wide smile.

"I thought it was thieves," he said.

"So we are," said Mama forking a sausage onto a plate. "Kitchen thieves."

"They smell good," Brad said, sniffing.

"I'll cook you some." I took two of the cold sausages from the greaseproof paper, prodded them with the fork to prevent the skins from bursting, and put them in the already hot pan. They sizzled and smelt delicious.

The kitchen door opened again and towheaded Sandor peered around.

I put another sausage in the frying pan.

Sandor said, "In the hostel in London, they fried bread with sausages. I liked that."

I cut a slice from the loaf on the drainboard by the sink and dropped it in the pan with the sausages.

Then we stood around the table, overcoats over our night clothes, and ate the sausages with our fingers.

CHAPTER THREE

THE NEXT morning, despite her interrupted night, Mama must have been up well before dawn, for she woke me with a cup of tea at half-past seven and had, I learned later, already scrubbed the floor and paintwork of the kitchen.

"It is English to wake with a cup of tea," she said after she had kissed me good morning. "So here is your English cup of tea."

Mama had on some overalls and had wrapped her lovely hair in a duster, tying it up in front above her forehead. I envied Mama her hair, which she kept long and parted in the middle, plaiting the ends and bringing them around each side of her head, or in a bun which rested delicately at the nape of her neck. This morning her eyes were bright and eager, and her beautiful hands were red from the scrubbing she had done. She had a happy smile about her lips and a smudge on the tip of her nose. And as I looked at her then, I felt one of those floods of love for her come sweeping over me.

"This morning," she said, sitting at the foot of my bed, "we will scrub and clean the dining room. If we have time, we will make a start on the bedrooms. Do you agree, sweetheart?"

Sipping the hot sweet tea, which I enjoyed, I nodded vigorously.

"Then this afternoon we have to visit the education people. You and Brad must both take a test to see if you are good enough for their grammar school. That has to be arranged." She stood up. "Now I get breakfast. Brad is in the bathroom."

I finished my tea and thought of the idea that had come to me.

I heard Brad moving along the passage from the bathroom. I called to him. He came into my room, his face red and shining and bright from soap and water.

"Brr," he said. "The water's cold. I must get the boiler in the kitchen going for hot water—if it will work. Did you sleep well?"

"Mm," I answered. "Brad, I've been thinking."

Brad nodded seriously. "So," he said. "It's good for the brain."

"Seriously. Mama—last night—sleeping on the floor. She mustn't sleep on the floor tonight."

My brother grinned. "She won't," he said. "I've already moved the bed from my room into hers and changed the bedclothes. She doesn't know. I did it as soon as she brought me my cup of tea—some time before she woke *you*. I let my tea get cold doing it."

I jumped out of bed and hugged him. "Poor, hard-done-by Brad," I said. "But I think you're not a bad brother to have. But—I'll tell you what. We'll take turns at sleeping in this bed. You one night, me the next."

Brad kissed my cheek. "Thank you, but it's not necessary. It won't do me any harm to sleep on the floor for a little while. And it won't be long before we can get another bed—you'll see."

I tried to argue, but he wouldn't listen.

"All right then," I agreed. "But I want Mama to have this wardrobe in her room."

"I'll help you move it," said Brad.

When we had done that and Brad had gone downstairs, I took down the curtains Mama had put in my room and took them along to hers. They didn't quite fit her window, but I put them up anyway, and they looked better than nothing.

Brad was right—the water *was* cold for washing, and it made me realize how sharp the morning was. I dressed quickly and then stood for a while looking out of my window. It was a gray morning, and the mist hung low over the marsh. I could not see the top of the lighthouse at the mouth of the creek as I had the previous evening. To the left of the marsh side of the garden stood the ruins of Chadhaven Castle, gaunt and wreathed in the mist that thickened and cleared all the time to every breath of the light breeze blowing in from the sea across the marshes.

Nothing could be seen clearly, and everything seemed to have had the color drained from it by the clinging gray mist. My spirits sank again—I felt gray and able to see nothing clearly.

Mama called up from the kitchen that breakfast was ready. I turned from the window and went downstairs, meeting Sandor on the way. He was rubbing his eyes, having been wakened only then by Mama's voice. He had his overcoat on over his pajamas and had put his shoes on his bare feet.

"Go back to bed, Sandor, sweet, if you are still sleepy," I told him.

"Mama called for breakfast," he answered, his voice still hoarse from sleep. "And I'm hungry, anyway."

We had breakfast, and then we all set to work. We worked hard that morning and cleaned and scrubbed the dining room and two bedrooms until the floors and the old paintwork shone as they had not shone for many years. When we had finished, and before we cleaned ourselves for lunch, Brad, Sandor, and I went out into the garden to explore.

The house was built in the shape of a thick L, with the long side of the L facing the marsh. The garden was quite large, and in the corner nearest the castle, which was on the other side of our hedge, was what had once been a tennis court. Toward the rear of the house there were six or seven trees, and right at the back of the house, before the hedge separating us from the people next door, was an overgrown kitchen garden. The rest of the garden—much of it must have been lawn—was also overgrown, and the grass was tangled and thick and nearly knee-high. Between the low garden wall separating us from the marshland and the marsh reeds themselves, there was a thin strip of sandy, clay-like, pebbly beach.

Brad and Sandor were thrilled with the size of the garden, the castle next door, and the marsh that spread, whispering and mysterious, between us and the sea. I was in the sort of mood that refuses to be thrilled by anything.

Brad was particularly happy because, in a tumble-down old outhouse built right in the corner among the trees, he and Sandor had found a number of things that, he said, would be of help in putting the house right. I didn't bother to go in.

The sight of the house next door, built in exactly the same style as ours but standing wonderfully cared for in a delightfully kept garden, made me feel that it was hopeless for us to think we could ever make anything of our old ruin. They had a tennis court and a small swimming pool—so Brad, who climbed on the ruined wall of the outhouse to see, told me. But, then, they were English; they had never known trouble or danger; they were rich and self-satisfied, and I hated them.

We moved toward the overgrown kitchen garden

and stood silently near the thick dividing hedge, looking toward our house across the weed-choked area that had once provided enough vegetables to keep the household. A half-rotten old wheelbarrow minus its wheel lay forlornly on its side nearby.

Brad was about to say something, when there came the crunch of footsteps on a gravel path on the other side of the hedge and the sound of laughter. Brad shrugged, and we started to move away, not wanting whoever it was from the house next door to overhear what we might say, for no other reason than that they were strangers and that our fleeting introduction to them had not been pleasant.

And then one of the laughing voices said, "Well, I'd scarcely got the words out of my mouth, when suddenly this redheaded fury sprang from nowhere and clouted me a right one, slap across the face. I was so surprised, the smack didn't begin to hurt until she was out of sight next door."

There was more laughter, and the footsteps came to a halt. The same voice went on, "These are the nettles, Stan. If you look at the undersides of the leaves you'll see the eggs there. And in June we'll have three or four of the most gorgeous peacock butterflies fluttering about the garden."

A second voice said, "Mm." There was a pause, and the second voice spoke again. "Are they really a crummy lot? Arthur Stevens said he saw a sort of caravan of old suitcases and parcels and a down-at-heel lot sloping along the quay yesterday afternoon. Would that be them?"

"That's them, all right. And to think because of them the Junior Sailing Club has been done out of an ideal clubhouse and headquarters. It makes you sick. Surely we've got enough problems in this country without letting in all the riffraff from some broken-down European country to lounge about and live on money our people pay in rates and taxes?"

"But what right had the town council to sell it to them anyway?"

"No right at all, Dad says, and he's going to kick up a stink about it. With a bit of luck we may be able to get the blighters out—by proving that the town council had no right to sell it to them."

"They had enough money to buy it, then?"

"Huh! Probably scrounged the deposit and got the rest on some sort of mortgage. Though goodness knows who would be fool enough to lend money to a woman like that. And they'll probably live on National Assistance."

I have never seen Brad move so quickly. He jumped onto the rickety old barrow and from there launched himself over the top of the hedge. He hit the top and, in a shower of snapping twigs and falling evergreen leaves, landed in a heap on the other side.

I ran along the path by the hedge and out of our front gate, along the road and into the open gateway next door, followed by Sandor. By the time I had run up the gravel path leading deep into next door's garden by the hedge, Brad and the boy whose face I'd smacked the day before were a mass of tangled arms and legs on the ground. Brad was not as old or as big as the boy he was fighting. The shock of his attack, however, had obviously taken the bigger boy very much by surprise, for he was on his back on the gravel path and Brad was sprawled astride him, pounding at him furiously. Another boy was there, pulling at Brad, trying to drag him from the boy on the ground.

I sprang at the boy pulling at Brad and grabbed a handful of his hair. With a startled yowl he left Brad and swung round to defend himself. Sandor limped to my aid, holding the boy's legs with his arms and hugging tight so that, what with my attack at his head and Sandor's attack at his legs, he stumbled and lurched to the ground too.

By now the strength of the boy from next door had told on Brad, and when I looked up from my own private war their positions were reversed. I left our victim, with Sandor still doggedly holding onto his legs, and dived at the boy punishing Brad. I was conscious of grabbing a handful of wiry brown hair, and then a swinging fist caught me on the side of my face. It hurt horribly, but I still kept hold of the hair and lashed out with my free hand.

I was half-blinded by tears, which were the result of a mixture of anger, pain, and humiliation, and was about to launch myself desperately into a new attack on the object of my hate, when I felt a firm hand grasp my arm. Another large, strong hand loomed into my vision and grasped with far more firmness the scruff of the neck of the boy who was still flailing his fists at Brad. I struggled against the restraining hand to no avail, and, at the same time, like a puppet whipped up and off the stage by invisible strings, the boy from next door was lifted clear of Brad and was deposited in an untidy heap about a yard away.

I turned, tensed and ready to fight some more, my eyes drowned in tears and my hateful red hair over my forehead and face. A man held my arm—a tall man whose face looked grim.

Now Brad was on his feet again; as he dived toward the boy on the ground, the man, still holding my arm, moved incredibly fast—half dragging me for about a yard—and grasped Brad by his arm. Brad turned a surprised red face, unable to believe that his onslaught could have been so quickly halted.

For a moment we all seemed frozen. Then the man said, "What in the name of heaven is this all about?"

I pointed to the boy Brad had attacked. "He said wicked things about our mother. Yesterday he said wicked things about all of us."

The man's grim expression did not relax. He said, "Ah, so you are the family who have taken over 'Light View,' are you?"

There was a defiant note in Brad's voice as he answered, "My mother has *bought* the place. Not as *he* said—with money borrowed which she'll never pay back—but with my father's money, which his books earned in this country."

I shook my arm free of the man's hand with a sudden violent movement. I said, "And yesterday he called us crummy refugees. Don't think I want to live here—I hate this place, and I hate the people here as well!"

The man looked from me to the boy Brad had jumped at. "Is this true, Phil? Did you say these things?"

"Oh, don't believe us," I burst in passionately. "We're only crummy refugees!"

"Please be quiet, young lady," said the man. "I'm asking my son a question—and I expect an answer from him."

I looked at the boy, who was now on his feet. He was a head taller than Brad, and oddly enough he had the same sort of wiry hair as Brad's, except that the English boy's hair was brown. He had blue eyes and thick, dark eyebrows. His jaw was square and his rather large mouth was set now in a tight line. I noticed that one of his eyes was bruised and turning a lovely black.

"I'm waiting for an answer, Phil," the man said again. "Did you say these things?"

"I suppose I did."

The man released Brad. To his son he said, "Then you brought anything that happened on yourself." The man turned to Brad and me. "As for you two young people," he said, "I apologize for my son's extreme rudeness. But I should be obliged if you would not trespass any more on my property."

I now noticed that one of Brad's eyes was also bruised and blackened, and I became conscious of the way he and Sandor and I were dressed. We were still in the old clothes we had put on to help Mama. We hadn't stopped to wash before we took our walk around the garden. The boy called Phil and his friend were dressed in school uniforms, black jackets with a beautiful red-and-gold badge—an old ship with a crown at the top of the tallest mast and what I took for a sea gull hovering in flight over the crown—on the breast pocket and long gray-flannel trousers. We were in old jeans—the boys were wearing shirts and I was in a jumper—dusty, smudged with dirt, and with grime on our hands and faces.

Yesterday this would have been too much for me, and I would probably have turned and fled. Today, despite my feeling of hopelessness, it was different. I took hold of Sandor's hand and turned to our neighbor.

"We had no wish to trespass in the first place. My brother did what any boy would have done hearing his mother spoken of as your son spoke of ours. There's just one thing I have to say before we go. I understand you are going to try and get us out of our house so that your petty sailing club can have it. For me you could have the place—I'd like nothing better than to leave here and leave this nasty little town for good. But for Mama's—my mother's—sake, because she wants it, I shall help her make a home of it. And neither you nor anyone else shall take it away from her."

It was the longest and angriest speech I had ever made, and I was breathless and trembling when I'd finished. I turned and walked swiftly away, almost pulling little Sandor with me, while Brad followed with determined steps.

He caught up with us in the road. "Sondra," he said, "that was marvelous. What a speech!"

"We won't say anything to Mama about this," I said, still breathless and trembling. "She's not to be worried."

"How about Brad's black eye?" asked Sandor. "How shall we say he got it?"

Brad felt the discolored, swollen skin around his left eye tenderly. "Ooh," he said, "it feels a real whopper."

"We'll have to tell a white lie." I was determined Mama should not know of this second incident. "You bumped into something in the old outbuilding, Brad."

"Let's just say I bumped into something, without saying where. We wouldn't be telling a lie then. For I *did* bump into something. The fact that it was someone's fist needn't bother Mama."

Sandor said with a worried frown on his face as we turned in at our gateway, "Sondra, could they really take our house away from us?"

Brad and I exchanged looks. Then I put my arm

around Sandor's thin little shoulders. "Of course they can't," I told him. "And they know it."

But that wasn't the way Brad and I saw it. In our experience, people in authority could do anything, and generally what they did was unpleasant.

CHAPTER FOUR

MAMA ACCEPTED our explanation of how Brad got his black eye, but I had to think fast to explain the slight bruise I had on my cheek. "It must have been while I was scrubbing, Mama. Though I didn't notice. We've been so busy. . . . Anyway, I bruise easily, and it couldn't have been much of a knock if I didn't notice it."

"Suddenly my children are all bumps and bruises." Mama smiled and looked at Sandor. "Haven't you got any wounds to show for your hard work this morning, my darling?"

"Well, Mama, no," answered Sandor seriously. "But then maybe I haven't worked as hard as Sondra and Brad."

We finished our lunch, cleaned ourselves, and dressed in the best clothes we had. Mama had pressed these while we had been getting rid of the dirt and grime we had collected during the morning.

By three o'clock Mama, Brad, and I were walking

into the grounds of Chadhaven King Edward Grammar School. We had left Sandor behind at his own request. He wanted to explore the garden more thoroughly and look at the ruined castle on the other side of the hedge. He would have been bored waiting for us during the interviews, and anyway he was sensible enough and amply self-reliant to be left on his own for a while.

A long, straight, neatly graveled road led from the decorative wrought-iron entrance gates to the school buildings. On either side stretched the school playing fields, and ahead stood the original school buildings, now many hundreds of years old. But there were larger, modern buildings on either side, and these housed on one side the boys' school and on the other, the girls'. Mama knew her way: she had been to see the headmaster of the combined school on her earlier visits to Chadhaven. We had arrived punctually, and the headmaster's secretary was waiting to take us in to him.

Both Brad and I were nervous. We knew that we were being thoroughly inspected to see if we were suitable for the school, even assuming we passed our scholastic test with honors. And I don't think it was the thought of being under the eye of Dr. Haisman, the headmaster, that was entirely responsible for our nervousness. It was Mama, with her supreme confidence in our ability to overcome every difficulty—scholastic and otherwise—that worried us a little. Supposing we failed and let her down?

However, there was little cause for us to have been

nervous as far as Dr. Haisman was concerned. But we weren't to know then that this somewhat craggy-faced man, with the almost crew-cut, iron-gray hair, the bull-like neck, and the immensely broad shoulders, was a man of compassion and kindness. His scraggy face hid it well, but we had a hint of it that very afternoon.

He welcomed Mama warmly and then sat her in the most comfortable chair in the room. He took off his thick-framed glasses and then asked Brad and me a number of very searching questions to find out, I suppose, how intelligent we were, how well we spoke and understood English, and what our scholastic standards were. Then he talked to us in French, which we both spoke fluently. He was smiling as he asked Brad how he had come by his black eye, and his smile broadened as Brad answered that he bumped into something in the garden.

When he had finished, he turned to Mama and smiled. "They should both do well in the entrance examinations, Mrs. Kopchek," he said. "You do understand there are four free places and four places with what we call assisted scholarships?"

Mama nodded.

Dr. Haisman went on: "There were a number of things I didn't explain on your two previous visits to me. This is not a school which is run by the country's education authorities. It was founded and endowed some four hundred years ago in the reign of Edward VI by private citizens. Most of the children are here because they have passed a common entrance examination, and their parents pay fees. But we have eight endowed scholarships. Four, as I have said, enable four children to attend the school without any payment, and in the other cases, quite a substantial contribution is made toward the fees. Do you understand?" Once more he smiled.

Mama nodded again. "I understand too that you are being very good in allowing my daughter and son to attempt the examinations, since they were held some months ago; also that Sondra and Bradislav are much older than the usual age at which children are accepted for your school."

"They haven't yet been accepted, Mrs. Kopchek. And I can only allow them to sit for tests now because in last year's examinations only two of the four free scholarships were awarded, as the standard required wasn't reached. But now . . . I think I would like to talk to you all. I think you are the sort of family who would like to know how everything stands."

Mama raised her eyebrows. "Ah? So?"

"Mrs. Kopchek, my decision to allow your children the chance of entering the school has met with quite a lot of opposition. I suppose it is understandable to a certain extent, seeing that each year something like four hundred children sit for those eight places. I have been taken to task by various town notables for allowing Sondra and Bradislav even to sit a specially set examination to suit their age—a more difficult examination than the one normally set. There are also some members of my staff who do not like this arrangement, but fortunately I have complete freedom and the last word in this matter."

The feeling of bitter resentment that had kept coming to me during these past weeks came again. They did not want us to have the house; now they didn't want us to have places in their school.

Dr. Haisman put his glasses on again. "In this instance their opinions are of no importance. I believe passionately that I am doing the right thing. If Sondra and Bradislav attain a standard of marking that, on comparison, brings them among the first eight places, then they will be given places in the school."

He looked at Brad and me and smiled. "I would like you both to report here at ten o'clock on Monday morning to take your exams. Sondra, you will sit your paper under the eagle eye of Miss Fraser. Bradislav, Mr. Stern will watch over you."

Dr. Haisman stood up. "I have, of course, heard the talk about your house and the ill feeling of part of the community over that. I am sorry that such a feeling should have made itself apparent to you in the way I believe it has. Unfortunately, I have the feeling that more is to be made of things I have mentioned, and I want you all to know I stand against the narrowness that opposes your having the chance to start a new life and that if I can help you in any way at all, I shall look upon it as an honor to do so."

Mama was smiling. "What you have said, Doctor, makes me happy. For what you are doing for us, I don't have enough English words to say thank you as I would like. What you are doing is wonderful for us. For the rest—we *must* face these difficulties and differences on our own. And overcome them on our own. We shall—you will see."

Dr. Haisman showed us out of his room and walked with us along the corridor toward the hallway opening from the main entrance to the old building. As we turned into the hall, a figure almost running collided with me, and we both staggered and fell. In the moment we squatted on the floor facing each other and before Dr. Haisman, Mama, and Brad helped us to our feet, I saw the startled eye-blackened face of the boy next door.

"Well, Cranstone," said Dr. Haisman, "you seem to be struck dumb by this brief encounter. I think you owe this young lady a large-sized apology. You really should not travel at such a speed indoors."

So our neighbors were called Cranstone.

He said, "I'm sorry, sir. I have a message for you from Mr. Soames, sir."

"You can deliver it in my office, Cranstone." Dr. Haisman turned to Mama and said, "Mrs. Kopchek, this is Philip Cranstone—our head boy—and, of course, his family are your neighbors."

Mama smiled and said, "How do you do?"

Dr. Haisman's eyebrows rose as his eyes went from Phil Cranstone to Brad. "Well I never," he said. "What a fine pair of matching black eyes we have here. How did you get yours, Cranstone?"

"I . . . er . . . stepped on the . . . er . . . garden rake this lunchtime, sir."

"Remarkable," said Dr. Haisman. "Young Kopchek here did something very similar. You bumped into something in the garden, didn't you, Kopchek?"

I warmed suddenly to Dr. Haisman for the way he spoke to Brad—addressing him in exactly the same way—as if Brad were already a member of the school. I could see Brad felt as I did.

"Yes, sir," he said.

One of Mama's eyebrows, I noticed, was raised. I envied Mama this ability to raise one eyebrow at a time. It looked very attractive on her. And it had a meaning too. When something dawned on Mama, when she solved some problem or other, she would raise one eyebrow. It seemed that both Mama and Dr. Haisman had put two black eyes together and made one fight out of them.

The subject was explored no further, however, because Dr. Haisman said, "Well, now, Cranstone, make your apologies to Miss Kopchek, and then please wait for me in my office."

Philip Cranstone went very red. I could see he was hating every second, and I didn't make it easier for him.

I looked at him wide-eyed and direct—you could say I was staring at him. And *I* was enjoying every second of it.

He said, trying to rush the words away from him, "I'm sorry to have knocked you down."

I said nothing.

"Mm, well, yes," said Dr. Haisman. "Come along, then, Mrs. Kopchek. I'll see you on your way, and we'll be looking forward to seeing Sondra and Bradislav on Monday."

At the steps he shook hands with Mama and said again, "Be patient with us, Mrs. Kopchek."

Mama said, "The patience mustn't be all on one side, Doctor. You will have to be patient with us too. Very patient."

As we reached the lovely wrought-iron gates at the entrance to the school grounds, Mama turned. Dr. Haisman was still standing on the steps of the Old School, a small figure all that distance away. When he saw Mama turn, he waved, and Mama waved back. Something told me that Dr. Haisman already admired Mama very much. And I knew that Mama felt a deep gratitude to him for the way he was trying to help us. For the first time that I could remember, I felt a warmth for someone outside my own family. Until that moment, I had not realized how alone we Kopcheks had always seemed to be. Even more so in our old country.

Mama did not speak until we were halfway home. Then she said, "Dr. Haisman is a *good* man." And almost immediately she followed this up with, "The trouble between both of you and that Philip Cranstone must stop. Already in two days Brad and he have given each other black eyes, and Sondra has slapped his face. I'm telling you, my darlings, there must be no more of it. I am not going to ask you to promise me this, but I want you to remember what I have said. There must be no more of it. Yes?"

Brad said, "Yes, Mama," which might have meant anything.

I didn't speak.

As we turned onto the lovely grass space of the quay to cut across to our house, a car—traveling much too fast for the rough grit road—swung around and pulled up outside the Cranstones' gateway.

A white-faced woman stood there, and the man who got out of the car was Mr. Cranstone. We heard the woman say in an anguished, high-pitched voice, "Oh, Mr. Cranstone. I can't think where she could have gone—or when. Debbie has never run off like this before."

Mr. Cranstone said, "Try not to worry, Mrs. Gibbs. I telephoned the police as soon as you got on to me at the boatyard. She can't have gone far. Most of the people in the district know her, and a four-year-old on her own in the town would soon attract attention."

"It's not the town I'm worried about," said the woman. "It's the river—or them marshes."

They were standing on the pathway as we came up

to them, and Mama stepped into the road so as not to have to squeeze between them and the car.

Mr. Cranstone's face was very different from when I saw it last—at lunchtime. Then it had been flushed with anger. Now it seemed drained of blood, drawn and taut with anxiety.

Mama half hesitated, as if she would speak, but Mr. Cranstone was so drowned in his worry that he didn't notice any of us and spoke again to the woman he had called Mrs. Gibbs. "You've searched everywhere—thoroughly?"

"Of course I have." Poor Mrs. Gibbs seemed about to burst into tears. "I've searched high and low. I love your daughter as if she were my own, Mr. Cranstone."

He patted her shoulder and started to walk her back to the house. "There, there, Mrs. G. I know that. Come on, let's get back to the house. The police will be sending someone along in a minute or two. Come and make me a cup of tea . . ."

His voice faded as they walked up the garden to the house, and we continued to walk toward "Light View."

Mama said, "It seems our neighbor has a baby daughter. . . . And his wife? Not at the house, anyway, today. That woman spoke of the river. . . . There should be railings. Oh, the poor baby, if she has fallen into the river!"

Mama was beginning to get as upset as Mrs. Gibbs had been.

"Please, Mama," I said. "The child may only have

gone into the town. You heard Mr. Cranstone say the police would be coming. They will probably bring the child with them."

"But there should be railings at the quayside," insisted Mama. Already her pace had quickened as we turned in at our gateway, and I could tell how her mind was working. Worried by the possible tragedy that might have befallen the people next door, she wanted to hurry to little Sandor, to reassure herself that he was safe.

She was calling his name before we were halfway up the path toward the house.

I looked over to one of the large but not unattractive boatyard buildings and at the sign above it which read: "F. Cranstone, Ltd., Boatbuilder."

I said to Brad, "If a child fell into the river from here, surely some workmen over in the boatyards would see it?"

"I should think so," said Brad. "But . . . I don't know. . . . It's difficult to say."

"It would be horrible if that's what has happened."

Brad looked at me slyly as we went into the house. "Ah, so. Our Sondra isn't the hardhearted fury she would have the Cranstones think she is."

"That's a stupid remark, Brad."

We heard Mama calling Sandor's name upstairs. There was no reply to her lonely, echoing call, and suddenly I felt a clutch of fear. "Oh, Brad," I whispered.

The door of the dining room was open where Mama had looked in for Sandor.

"Don't be silly," said Brad. "Getting lost's not an epidemic—it's not catching. He's probably still exploring the castle. I'll go and see if I can find him."

Mama came down as Brad left the house. "I know I'm being foolish, Sondra. Sandor is out having fun somewhere. But that little baby from next door . . ."

"Brad's gone to fetch him, Mama. Sandor *did* say he wanted to explore the castle and round about. And you know Sandor's a very sensible boy."

"But so young—and so little." Mama's face was tight, her voice unsure. She walked to the kitchen. "I'm going to do what the English do in a crisis," she said. "I'm going to make a cup of tea."

I tried to make a joke. "Anyway it's tea time," I said, following her into the kitchen. "So it's time to make tea."

Mama sniffed—to stop herself from crying, I thought. "Stop trying to stop me acting as the English," she said. She put the kettle on, crying softly over the match as she struck it, and lit the gas.

Brad ran through the back door and along the short passage to the kitchen. "Mama," he called softly. "You'd better come."

"Blessed heaven!" cried Mama, dropping the box of matches on the floor and following Brad, who had turned back to the garden at a run. "What now?"

I followed, fear gnawing at my heart again. I caught up with them as they reached the old tumble-down brick shed among the trees.

Mama and I peered in as Brad stepped aside and indicated where we should look.

Sandor was there. And so was a little girl about four years old. They were both asleep. It appeared as if they had been looking at picture books together, for a pile of them lay beside them, and one, which was open, lay across Sandor's legs.

He was sitting on some old sacking with his back against some crates. The little girl was sitting beside him. It seemed that she had fallen asleep first, for her dark, tousled head was nestled on Sandor's shoulder and rested close to his neck. His arm was around her waist, and she slept there secure in the comfort of that small, thin arm. It looked as if Sandor had gone on reading for a while until he too had dropped off to sleep in the shelter of the old shed.

Mama said softly, almost to herself, as if we weren't there, "Ah, so. . . . When my eyes see such a sight, then I *know* that God is good."

CHAPTER FIVE

Mama went into the shed and gently disturbed the two sleepers. Sandor woke fairly easily and immediately looked a little sheepish at being caught sleeping in the afternoon. Mama lifted Deborah in her arms, and the baby opened her eyes, smiled at Mama, and was quite prepared to snuggle down again and go back to sleep.

"Come along, darling," Mama said. "Your daddy is looking for you. He's worried—he thought he had lost his baby."

The child opened her eyes and sat up. She looked at Mama as if she thought all grownups were idiots and said, as if it explained everything, "Debbie with Sandor." Then she smiled down at Sandor.

Mama said, "Ah, so! Already my youngest son has made a conquest. Pick up the books, darling, and bring them along. We must take Debbie home."

Mama and Sandor were gone only a very short time, and when they returned, Mama's face, I thought, was set. I was making the tea, and I walked from the kitchen to the dining room, where Mama had come in to sit down, and looked out of the bare windows.

"Were they pleased to get their baby back?" I asked.

Mama smiled. "How could they not be?" she answered.

"And did they thank you nicely?" There was acid in my voice. "And ask you in?"

Sandor said, "The man said thank you, but he didn't say much else. He just took Debbie from Mama at the door and went in."

"He was worried and anxious, and the police were there. I would have been forgetful too if such a thing had happened to me."

"Huh!" I said. "There was nothing else to be expected from such a family."

"But Debbie's nice," said Sandor, a frown creasing his forehead. "She's only a baby, and she *is* nice."

Brad grinned at Sandor. "How did you two come to be such friends so suddenly?" he asked.

"She saw me exploring the garden," explained Sandor, "and we talked through the hedge. Then she brought her books around and asked me to read to her. And I did."

"*And* went to sleep," teased Brad.

"That was an accident," said Sandor. "I never meant to."

He looked at me a little defiantly. "I *like* Debbie. She's not like the others. She's only a baby."

"That's *it*." I spoke cruelly, scathingly, unable to help

myself from being so deliberately unkind. "She's only a baby—and you're a big boy of nine years. *Reading* to a baby!"

As soon as I saw Sandor's face I wished I had never said those words. I had hurt him. He'd been so proud of being able to read English books to a little English girl; he'd been so eager to make friends.

Mama looked at me with a raised eyebrow and put her arm around Sandor. "We're very proud of you being able to read so well." She kissed him.

Brad said, "You can already read English nearly as well as I can."

I was hating myself and feeling suddenly alone. I wanted to hug Sandor and say I was sorry for what I'd said, but I sat still, sullen and silent, wishing so desperately that I could get rid of this horrible feeling of shame, resentment, and hopelessness. At the slightest thing, the feeling seemed to take charge of me, and because of it I made myself and Mama and Brad and Sandor miserable.

I went out into the kitchen again and finished making the tea. Then I brought it in, and we were all silent for some time.

Brad and Sandor finished, kissed Mama, and went out to the outbuilding among the trees. Brad wanted to sort out all the stuff there that might be useful and separate it from the rubbish.

When they had gone, Mama said, "Our time of unhappiness is over, Sondra. Here *we* can make our lives what we will."

"If other people allow us. Look at what has just happened. The man couldn't even say thank you properly. I hate these people. They are cold and self-centered, and they don't want us. And they'll find a way of getting rid of us."

"No, no!" For the first time, Mama's voice was angry. "That is not so. *We* are masters of our own lives here. Whether we are happy or miserable is up to us. Remember that." She put her arm around my shoulders, and when she spoke again the anger had left her voice. "I know how you feel, darling. . . . I know most of the sort of things you feel. I'm your mother, and once upon a time—too many years ago—I was a girl of your age. Now I have one or two letters to write. Why don't you go and help Brad?"

I walked slowly all around the garden before I went up to the old outhouse among the trees. It was dusk now, and Brad and Sandor had been hard at work. Outside the outhouse were stacked many of the yellowy-gray roof slates with which the house was covered and a pile of odd lengths of timber. There were also some old paintpots and buckets.

Brad said, "If we had a ladder I could maybe repair the roof."

"You wouldn't know how," I said.

Brad looked at me. "There are many things I don't

know about repairing a house. But I'll find out. And I'll tell you what, Sondra. I'm not going about like a sick hen, clucking and moaning and feeling sorry for myself. It's time you got out of your moodiness."

"I'm not moody. I—" I stopped and turned away.

I was angry, more with myself than Brad, because I knew he was right. *Why* did I have this feeling of hopelessness, when the rest of the family were eager to go forward and build a new life? I turned back to Brad and put a hand on his arm.

"Brad—I'm sorry. . . . I don't know what . . . It's just that everything seems so huge and always against us. Forgive me?"

He put his arms around my shoulder. "I've nothing to forgive, Sondra . . . but if you could show Mama . . . you know?"

I nodded and bent and kissed Sandor. "I'm sorry to you too, sweetheart—for being unkind about Debbie."

Sandor hugged me. "I knew you didn't mean it," he said, "when you said it."

It was nearly dark now, and we all turned and walked slowly back to the empty house. No—it wasn't empty, for Mama was there.

For the first time since we had arrived in England, I felt the weight that seemed to be pulling my heart down lift and go away.

The following morning, Mama left the house early. "I'm looking for work," she told us gaily, and went.

Brad and I sat down and spent some time planning how we should repair and redecorate the house—once we had some money to buy paint. I hadn't realized how many things we should need before we could even start. Brad's list of paintbrushes and other tools—the names of which I promptly forgot—seemed to be unending. And all would cost money.

Yesterday this would have sent me into another depressed mood. Today it seemed to be a challenge. Mama's unconquerable spirit and Brad's fierce loyalty to her had finally broken through my attitude. Brad and I, helped by Sandor, cleaned two more rooms before Mama returned at lunchtime—gay, triumphant. She had found work and was to start on Monday. Her job, she told us, was as caretaker of Chad Hall, which was a building in the town used for public meetings, dances, and other functions. I felt a momentary pang. Caretaker—when Mama had been a university graduate in our old country. But Mama was happy about her job. We finished scrubbing the rest of the rooms—except the attics, which we decided not to do until the roof had been repaired.

On Sunday, we gaily started to strip the old paper from the walls of one of the bedrooms. Our enthusiasm lessened as the difficulties became more apparent. We had no proper tools to scrape the paper from the walls, and the floors which we had so painstakingly scrubbed became dirty again and covered with paper and dust from the walls.

We saw our mistake when we had done only a quarter

of the room. We all felt a little silly because no one had thought of the mess the job would make—the paper scraping should have been done first. We laughed, stopped working, cleaned ourselves, and had some food. In the afternoon we walked along the foreshore, past the castle, over a footbridge crossing a brook that ran into Broad Creek. We passed the edge of a wood which stretched down to the marsh and from which herons occasionally flapped from the trees to fly to the creeks. We walked along to where Heron Creek started, then we turned and made for home.

That night Mama persuaded Brad and me to go to bed earlier than usual because of our test the following day.

We were all up early that Monday morning. Mama had to be at Chad Hall by eight, and Sandor had to be taken to the primary school that she had arranged for him to attend. On the following days, he would be able to go on his own, but on his first day, Brad and I, who were not due at the grammar school to start our examinations until ten o'clock, took him.

We were received by a rather straight-faced man, Mr. Dangerfield, the headmaster of the school. After saying in a sort of parrot way that he thought Sandor would do well and that he was sure he would be happy at the school, Mr. Dangerfield led Sandor away to join a class of other nine-year-olds, whom we had seen playing noisily in the school playground before the bell rang.

I was glad Mama was not there. The sight of Sandor limping along at the side of the thickset, humorless schoolmaster struck me as pathetic. He was about to be pushed into an alien world, and none of us would be there to give him strength and encouragement. He walked along the cold, bare corridor, and there were tears on my cheeks as Brad took my arm.

Outside I sniffed and blew my nose and smiled at Brad. I said, "But he looked so small—so alone."

"He did, didn't he? But you know, Sondra, I think Sandor has a great deal of Mama's strength and courage in him. More maybe than either you or I."

We were at the grammar school by a quarter to ten and were welcomed by Dr. Haisman himself. How kind he was, and how he tried to put us at ease. Brad went off to an anteroom to start his exam, and I was taken to another by Miss Fraser, a young woman of about twenty-six who, like me, was redheaded and who wore attractive upswept glasses. She was pretty and freckled and seemed ready to smile at the first opportunity if there was anything worth smiling at.

I felt nervous and kept wanting to yawn during the time paper, ink, and pens were being laid out and the first question paper brought. And my hands were unsteady too. But once the questions were before me, I tried to push everything from my mind and concentrate.

Monday went and so did Tuesday, when we completed the last two papers, and in the evening we compared notes as we had the night before. Brad and I both felt we hadn't done too badly. Mama was sure we had done famously. Sandor now reported on his second day at school, and Mama bubbled about her job. She told us there would be quite a few evenings during the week when she would be late or have to go out to the Hall to see that everything was all right and lock up the place after meetings.

There were over three weeks to the end of the term, and we wouldn't know how we had fared in our examinations for at least another week. If we had succeeded, we wouldn't start school anyway until the beginning of the next term. Brad and I had time on our hands. On Wednesday morning, after Mama had left for work and Sandor had gone to school, Brad went out. I was glad, because I had a plan I wanted to put into operation. I wanted to try and find some sort of temporary work for myself so that I could earn some money toward my school uniform. I didn't see how Mama could possibly buy me that and feed us and buy the things we needed to decorate the house in the short time between now, the Easter holidays, and the start of the new term. And I would have hated having to go to the school not wearing the school uniform.

I had no idea of the sort of work I would be able to do, so I decided to walk around the town to explore the possibilities. When I got back to the house, Mama and

Brad were there, and the success of my morning's exploration must have been reflected on my face, for Brad said, "Sondra looks like she's found a gold mine in the garden."

They were in the kitchen, and Mama was preparing our light midday meal. "I got a job so that I can buy my school dresses and things," I said.

"What sort of a job?" Brad asked.

I leaned on the edge of the kitchen table, and Mama stood with her arm around my shoulder, smiling.

"Delivering newspapers. Every morning—Sundays as well—and I'm to be paid thirty shillings a week." I got it out all in one breath because I expected some opposition from Mama.

But she gave my shoulder a squeeze and said, "Then you'll have to buy yourself one of those maps of the town in the town guidebooks."

"Before school?" said Brad. "That means getting up early. Uh-uh! That's not for me. I'd rather have the sort of job *I've* got."

"No! *You* haven't been out searching for a job too?" I could feel a giggle coming.

Brad grinned and nodded. "I have—and I've got one. In the joinery shop of one of the boatyards. I go in every day after lunch and bag up all the sawdust and shavings. Bag up," added Brad with a deliberate pomposity in his voice, "means putting the sawdust and shavings into sacks. And when the men knock off—finish work for the day—at five o'clock, I sweep up the shop, get it ready for them to start the next morning. And they're going to give me two pounds a week."

I looked at Brad and smiled. "Brad!"

Mama came and put her arms around us, looking from one to the other.

"Now," she said, her voice just a little unsteady, "now we are ready to start building a wonderful, strong, and happy castle for the Kopcheks. With roots—deep roots."

CHAPTER SIX

I BOUGHT MY map of the town and started delivering the newspapers on Thursday, and Brad started at the boatyard the same afternoon. On Friday he came home with sixteen shillings for his two afternoons' work, and on Saturday morning Mrs. Poplin—the large, fat, waddling woman who owned the news agent's—gave me seven and sixpence. We put the money in two small tins, and I helped Brad, who didn't have to work on Saturdays, scrape some more paper off the walls.

Those weeks before Easter were full of work for us—work which we all enjoyed. We were too busy to think of much else. From the money we earned—Mama, Brad, and I—we bought paint and brushes. We decided that wallpaper was too expensive, and we painted the walls of our rooms in bright yellows and pinks and the dining room in Wedgwood blue. We distempered the ceilings and painted the woodwork; for weeks on end, we lived with the smell of paint and were always spotted somewhere on our hands and faces with the latest color we had used.

By Easter we had done the dining room, the kitchen, and our three bedrooms, to say nothing of the bathroom. That left us three more rooms to do downstairs, three bedrooms on the first floor, and the two attics. Already the house seemed to have lifted up its head from its loneliness and the misery of being tumbledown. Somehow the dead stone seemed to come to life, as if it knew that someone loved and cared for it.

During this period, Mama contrived to buy some material to make curtains, and our bedrooms and the dining room no longer looked like bare caves with staring eyes. She had even stretched her money far enough to buy some lamp shades, and the rooms we used lost still further their bald, empty look.

And so Good Friday came and Mama declared a holiday. It was a soft April day. Hundreds of daffodils, which had pushed their determined way through the tangle of grass in the garden, gave warm splashes of color to our little wilderness.

Mama said, "We'll take our lunch and picnic." It was a wonderful idea, and we set out quite soon after breakfast. Loaded with food baskets, we made our way along the edge of the marsh—the way we had walked before. We disturbed moor hens and coots, who disappeared like scurrying black balls into the reeds and the safety of the water. A mallard waddled out of our path with a rather bad-tempered expression, outraged that he should have been disturbed. Mama laughed and said the mallard's waddle reminded her of Mr. Strake, who was a council official and who had something to do with the Hall, where she acted as caretaker.

We passed a swan on her nest on a minute island in the middle of the mud and water, about ten yards out in the marsh, and the cob, who had been browsing in the shallow water nearby, turned at our approach and paddled belligerently toward us, warning us to keep away. We crossed the small bridge spanning the stream that emptied its waters into Broad Creek and walked along the edge of the large wood, which I later learned was called the Heronry because of the number of herons that nested in its old, high trees. Blackbirds sang their sun song, and great tits sawed away everlastingly in their squeaky two-note cheeps. High above the trees, a wood lark fluttered and trilled, and from a branch in a tree up which a little tree creeper moved like a mouse, a chaffinch sang its repetitive five-note song.

We reached the beginning of Heron Creek, and on a stretch of tight turf sloping down toward a stream and the edge of the marsh, Mama stopped.

Brad said, "This is a good place, Mama."

Mama looked at Sandor, who had begun to tire. "Then here we stay. It's lovely," she agreed.

Behind us the ground sloped upward, thick with great trees; among them, big clusters of primroses patched the earth with yellow. The bank on which we sat was above the level of the tips of the reeds of the marsh, and we could look over them, unmoving now in the still air, to a stretch of blue beyond where the sea edged the horizon to merge with the sky. The long, low, smoke-smudged lines of a cargo vessel on its way to Minthampton moved incredibly slowly, it seemed, across the wide expanse of our vision. Nearer to us, gulls—a mixture of black-headed and black-backed—rode the air on beautifully spread wings.

We flopped to the ground and spread our tired legs.

"I'd like to explore the marshes among the reeds," said Sandor.

Brad smiled. "You'd need a flat-bottomed boat."

"Aren't there *any* dry paths, do you think?" I asked.

Brad shrugged. "I expect so. We must find out. Maybe one day we can get a small boat and explore the creeks."

"I bet there are lots of wild animals in the marshes," Sandor said in the tone of one who doesn't know but who hopes there are.

"Like tigers and elephants and black panthers and snakes and crocodiles," Brad grinned.

"You're an idiot, Brad. Isn't he, Mama? *He* knows what I mean. Like otters and voles and things like that." Sandor turned to look up into the woods behind. "Anyway, I bet there are badgers and foxes up in the woods."

I asked him, "How do *you* know all about badgers and otters and voles, anyway?"

"They were in Debbie's books," he answered, getting to his feet. "Mama, I'm going to see if I can find any—badgers, I mean."

"Well, don't frighten them if you find any, darling," Mama told him. "And don't get lost."

Sandor limped off happily and was soon out of sight among the trees. We sat quietly for some minutes, reveling in the warmth of the sun, the sight of the still reeds and the sea beyond.

Then Mama said, "Anyone should want to hear my plan?" Occasionally Mama still had slight difficulty in constructing her English. Especially if she were excited or happy.

Brad and I turned to look at her. "Plan? What plan?"

Mama smiled and hugged her knees. "In the summer," she said, "a lot of visitors come to Chadhaven for their holidays—to sail in small boats up and down in the water."

Brad leaned toward Mama and hugged her. "*On* the water, Mama. They're not in submarines."

"Up, down, in, out—what does it matter? They come for their holidays anyway. Now stop correcting me, who has a university degree in mathematics, and listen to my brain wave."

"Brain storm," corrected Brad gently. I giggled.

Mama threw up her hands and aimed her handkerchief at Brad. It missed and landed a little way down the slope.

"So," Mama said, "I'll keep my plan to myself." But we knew she just couldn't wait to get it out, so we were not worried. Brad rolled himself down the bank and retrieved Mama's handkerchief. He came back and handed it to her with an Old World flourish.

"Please tell us, Mama," he said. "We know you can't wait, and we can't bear to see you suffer."

Mama aimed a cuff at Brad, which he had no difficulty in dodging, and said, "Such a son I have!" Then she settled down to tell us her plan.

The owner of the smallest hotel in the town was new to Chadhaven just as we were. He had been in the place nearly a year, but he was still new enough to be a stranger. He had done some catering at the Hall, and afterward he and Mama got to talking about Chadhaven and other things. And it seemed that the preceding summer, when lots of visitors came to Chadhaven for sailing holidays or as tourists, he had been forced to turn people away because the hotel was full.

We were still mystified, and Mama knew it. Her eyes sparkled and her lips were trembling with the eargerness of a smile.

"The hotel is that one just behind the church," she said.

"Three or four minutes from us," said Brad. "I know it. It's called the Golden Anchor. But . . ."

Mama held up her hand. "This Bradislav Kopchek knows everything. Then perhaps he knows my plan?"

"Shut up, Brad, and let Mama finish," I said.

He grinned. "Women are a great trial to me."

"This is my plan, and I put it to Mr. Slater, who owns

the hotel. And after Easter, he is coming to see us and talk some more about it." Mama stopped and hugged her knees tighter, looking happy and excited but saying nothing. She was teasing us, waiting for us to get impatient. I bit my lip and tried to stop myself from smiling and bursting out with questions. But Brad obliged.

He got to his feet. "Mama—if you don't tell us right away what all this is about, I shall walk straight into the reeds of the marshes, never to be seen again." He stood there in a melodramatic attitude that was a cross between a third-rate actor registering desperation and an opera singer halfway through a fifteen-minute dying-swan aria.

The smile left Mama's face, and she shuddered. "I'll tell," she said. "Anything to stop you showing the world that acting is *not* in your blood."

At last we heard Mama's plan. It boiled down to this: If Mr. Slater had had an annex, he could have kept it filled with visitors. But there was no land available for expanding the hotel, and he felt he was missing the chance of making more money.

"Now, what I thought was this," Mama went on. "*We* could act as Mr. Slater's annex. We have many spare bedrooms, and all we would have to do would be to give the visitors early-morning tea. They would breakfast and eat all their other meals at the hotel."

"But what about furniture, Mama—we could never buy furniture for all those bedrooms." I felt a flatness after waiting for the plan. We had the bedrooms, yes. But they were completely empty.

"That's the beauty of my plan! Mr. Slater is coming to see the house, and if we can come to an agreement, he will furnish the rooms and I will pay him for the furniture and carpets and bed linen out of the money he would pay me for taking his overflow guests."

Now I sat up. This was exciting. It sounded like a wonderful way of furnishing the house and, later, making enough money so that maybe Mama wouldn't have to go out to work. We would be in business on our own account!

Brad was impressed too. "Mama, you're a genius."

"I know it," said Mama complacently.

I leaned over and kissed her cheek. "Mama, you're wonderful."

"But wait until Mr. Slater has been to see us," Mama said. "Maybe he won't like us when he sees us all. Maybe he won't like the house."

"He will! He will!" I was so excited. It was a wonderful idea. It couldn't fail. Life was suddenly brighter —with a real, immediate promise.

Brad said with a grin, "He'd better." Then he became serious and keen. "I could soon get the garden tidied. I could enlarge the vegetable garden—maybe we could grow enough fresh vegetables to sell some to Mr. Slater."

"From someone who has never even grown a flower in a pot," I said, "that sounds pretty ambitious."

Mama stretched. "We've still got to decorate the hall and the rest of the rooms, and all the outside painting has to be done. But we'll do it. Already we have done well for the short time we have been here. We . . ."

The sound of footsteps close by made us look up. We had expected to see Sandor, but instead it was a girl—the girl who had been with Philip Cranstone when I slapped his face. She stood there on the path just above us, looking at us with uncertainty. My smile disappeared, and Brad's mouth clamped shut.

Only Mama continued smiling as she looked at the girl, who finally, under the encouragement of that smile, spoke.

"I'm Sheila Cranstone," she said flushing. "I saw you leave this morning and came after you to speak to you."

Mama patted the grass by her side. "Come and sit here, my dear."

Brad looked out over the top of the tall reeds toward the sea. I continued to stare at Sheila Cranstone. She was about my age, with light-brown to fairish hair and large brown eyes set widely apart. Her nose was nicely shaped, and her mouth and chin had a softness about them that was entirely different from the cast of her brother's features. There was nothing insipid about the lines of her mouth, though, nor about the line of her chin. It was just that they seemed gentle to me. Not that that softened me toward her. She was quite nervous, standing there, and her long, slender fingers, which tapered to tastefully manicured nails, fiddled.

She didn't move from where she stood. "I—I just wanted to thank you, Mrs. Topchek—"

Mama's smile widened, "It's Kopchek—but it doesn't matter."

"Oh—I'm sorry." Sheila Cranstone flushed more deeply. "I—I wanted to thank you for bringing Debbie back. I—I've not had an opportunity before, and I'm afraid Daddy was . . . uh . . . a little abrupt. . . ."

"That's all right. He was . . . distrait?" Mama looked at me, query in her voice, her eyebrows raised.

"Distraught," I said shortly.

"Yes—distraught." Mama thanked me with a nod, happy to be able to show off my knowledge. "He was distraught. Debbie had been missing a long time already."

Sheila Cranstone turned to me. "I'd like to say I'm sorry for what you heard Phil—my brother—say the first day you arrived. We—we're not *really* like that. . . . You know—being English and looking down on all foreigners . . . and that sort of old-fashioned thing."

"It doesn't matter." I tried to sound indifferent.

Mama said again, "Come and sit by me, my dear. Don't stand way up there. I very much appreciate what you have said. Circumstances make people say things they otherwise wouldn't."

Brad got to his feet. "If you'll excuse me, Mama, I'll go try to find Sandor."

He started to move into the woods. I scrambled up. "I'll go with you." I didn't want Sheila Cranstone to sit down with us and spoil our party, and Mama looked as if she were about to invite her to join us for the rest of the day. I felt guilty as I hurried to catch up with Brad, and I didn't dare look at Mama, expecting her to call us back. But she didn't, and Brad and I went on in silence through the trees and were soon out of sight of the green bank.

After about twenty minutes, we found Sandor watching a large hole that an animal had dug out of a steeply rising knoll fairly well covered with bushes and saplings.

"Is it a fox's or a badger's?" asked Brad.

"I don't know," answered Sandor. "I was waiting to find out."

"You don't think a fox or a badger is going to come out in broad daylight, do you? And with your scent all around the place?"

"I don't smell."

Brad laughed. "You don't to us, but you do to them, believe me!"

"Come on, Sandor," I said. "Let's all three of us go exploring a little way."

We walked slowly among the trees, and as we went Sandor picked primroses. We reached the edge of the wood; beyond, a field rose up toward the rounded summit of one of the Quarr Hills. We disturbed a pair of partridges, and they whirred away from us in a flutter of urgent wings, flying low across the field. The suddenness of their flight gave us all a scare, and Sandor dropped his bunch of primroses and Brad and I had to help him gather them again. Then we made our way slowly back toward the other end of the wood at the edge of the marsh, to where Mama was sitting on the bank.

We had been away for almost an hour; when we returned, Brad and I were relieved to find Mama alone. I expected Mama to have a few words to say about our rudeness in going off as we did. But she said nothing as she moved about fixing our picnic lunch; she just looked up at us and smiled. Then she said, "You found Sandor, then? Hungry? I am."

When we were all seated eating our sandwiches she said, "I'm glad you two went off when you did. And so was Sheila, I should think."

"Now, Mama," I began.

Mama went on: "It gave her a chance to talk to me. You know—that Sheila Cranstone is a sweet girl. Poor dear—she's not very happy."

"I'm not surprised—with a father and a brother like that," I said.

Mama looked at me. "The whole family of them aren't so happy. Only Debbie seems to really enjoy life—but that's because she is too young to understand."

"Debbie," said Sandor, "is a nice little baby. She should be happy."

"But I still don't see what *any* of the Cranstones would have to say to us," said Brad.

"*Any* of the Cranstones didn't have *anything* to say

to us," answered Mama with ominous sweetness. "Only Sheila—to me. And what she had to say made me sad too. Sad for the Cranstones."

"Huh!" Brad grunted.

Mama finished her sandwich before she spoke again, and while she was eating I was dying to ask what it was Debbie wouldn't understand. But I crammed my mouth full to stop myself. This time Sandor came to my rescue. "What doesn't Debbie understand, Mama?"

"Well, my sweetheart," said Mama, "it just goes to show you don't have to be refugees like us to have been unhappy. And it may help you all to understand why . . . But I'm not going to preach you a sermon. I'm going to tell you a story—the story Sheila told me. Mrs. Cranstone died when Debbie was born. She was young and she died so suddenly and so unexpectedly that the force of the shock was multiplied tenfold. They were a happy family, and Sheila says her father has never really got over the shock. None of them have, but it's hit Mr. Cranstone worst of all."

"What does she tell us this for?" I said with some bitterness, remembering Father.

"Because she wants us to try and understand why her father and her brother are like they are."

Brad said quietly, "How old is Debbie? Four? Well, Father died much less than four years ago—just as suddenly and far more brutally. But we're not bitter toward people who had nothing to do with it."

This wasn't true—not of all of us. I remembered my feelings and actions. Mama looked at me—she knew what I was thinking.

"Well, anyway, Mr. Cranstone has flung himself into his work and has done a lot of work for the town," Mama said. "He and his son started the Chadhaven Junior Sailing Club, and they tried to get our house—before we were ever heard of here—as the club's headquarters. But the council said no. Then we came. And when I asked if I could buy it, the council said yes. Put yourselves in the Cranstones' place and then say honestly if you wouldn't have acted in the same way toward us as they have."

"Mama, you're too kind," I said.

Mama shrugged. "Sheila told me their story to try and make us see that her father and brother were not acting according to their real natures."

"She seems too good to be true." Brad was staring out toward the sea as he spoke.

Mama ignored his remark. "I think she wants us to realize that we could, if we were willing to try, change his attitude toward us."

"I agree with Brad," I said. "And as far as I'm concerned she's wasting her time."

CHAPTER SEVEN

Dressed in our best clothes, we all went to church on Easter Sunday morning. It was a hazy April day, more like summer than spring, and the inside of the church was gold and soft with daffodils and pussy willows in powder-puff bloom. The church was full and we sat at the back. We saw the Cranstones there—all of them except Debbie. After the service, Dr. Haisman joined us as we walked slowly through the churchyard. He talked to Mama for some minutes and then told us we should soon be hearing the results of our tests.

That afternoon we sat on the low wall of the garden fringing the marsh and made plans as to how we should complete the decoration of the house and the tidying up of the garden. Brad suggested that Mama and I concentrate on the inside and that he should work on the outside. He proposed to borrow a ladder from the boatyard where he had been working—Fryer's and Sons—to repair the roof and paint. Brad was determined to turn "Light View" into a living home. From wood he had found in the shed, he had made a very passable pair of steps, up which he climbed to distemper the ceilings. He had learned these things from a weekly do-it-yourself magazine that I delivered to him every Friday.

Mama agreed that it seemed a good idea, although she was not too happy at the thought of Brad going onto the roof.

We started work again on the house on Easter Monday, which was a gray, drizzly day anyway, and on Wednesday morning a letter arrived from Dr. Haisman informing Mama that Brad and I had been awarded the remaining two of last year's four free scholarships to the grammar school. Brad and I were delighted and a little surprised, but Mama received the news as though she had expected it. She merely put on her hat and raincoat and said, "And so we go to the school outfitters for your uniforms."

If we had known the enmity, the trouble leading almost to tragedy, our successes were to cause, we would not have been so happy as we were at that moment.

We took the money we had saved from the tin boxes and added it to Mama's purse. Then, feeling rather gay and a little apprehensive at the same time, we three made our way in the rain to the store in Fore Street that had the monopoly of supplying the uniforms for the school. Sandor chose to stay at home reading the one or two inexpensive books I had bought him from Mrs. Poplin's.

We'd seen the boys' uniform before—when we fought Phil Cranstone and his friend. The jacket was a black blazer with a red-and-gold badge of the school on the breast pocket—an old three-masted sailing ship with a crown above the tallest mast and, above the crown, a sea gull with outstretched wings. The cap was black with red-and-gold horizontal lines and a smaller replica of the badge in front. Gray-flannel trousers completed Brad's outfit. In another department of the store, I was fitted out with my summer uniform. This consisted of three pale-blue dresses with short sleeves and white collars. The sleeves were edged in white as well. The hats were of the straw-boater type with narrow brims, and around the crown of the hat was a red-and-gold ribbon, with the lovely badge in front. I was pleased with the way I looked when I tried it all on, while Mama sat and watched proudly. There were some adjustments to be made to my dresses, but Brad's blazer and trouser sizes were in stock, and we walked home carrying two smart-looking cardboard boxes containing his school clothes. Sumners, the school outfitters, was the most fashionable, as well as the oldest, store in the town. And the candy-striped boxes we carried helped balance for me the memory of that day when we had walked from the station with paper-wrapped parcels and tattered suitcases.

The drizzle had stopped, and Mama was gay as we walked—Brad and I on either side of her. We came to Moult's Coffee House. Mama stopped and said, "We'll have a small celebration. We will have morning coffee."

We went into Moult's and sat at a table in the bow window and drank coffee. Sheila Cranstone was sitting at a table with two other girls. She smiled and waved to Mama, and in the mood I was in at that moment I think I would have smiled back at her as Mama did, but when Sheila caught my eyes on her, she turned away as if she was embarrassed and went on talking to her friends.

We finished our coffee and went back home to find that Sandor had a visitor whom he was entertaining. Debbie Cranstone was sitting at the table in the dining room, listening with rapt attention while Sandor read to her from one of his new books.

Sandor looked up and smiled at us as we entered the room. "Hello, Mama."

Debbie dragged her mind away from the world of fantasy through which Sandor had been conducting her and smiled too. "Sandor's reading to me," she said. "About Ali—what's his name, Sandor?"

"Alidad the Water Seller," answered Sandor. "It's a good story about a boy who sold water from a goatskin in a far-off eastern land." Sandor was obviously quoting from the book.

Mama smiled at them both. "Well, enjoy your story." She went into the kitchen to prepare lunch, and Brad went off to the outhouse among the trees to unearth more old timber and stuff that might come in useful in our work in and about the house.

I sat down at the table with the two children for a few moments. Sandor hesitated. "Go on reading," I told him. "I'm only sitting for a minute."

"And so the Grand Vizier—"

"What's that?" asked Debbie.

Sandor looked at me helplessly. He didn't know either.

"A Grand Vizier was a Prime Minister," I said. "A very important man."

"Oh," said Sandor, and Debbie looked just as wise as before.

"And so the Grand Vizier . . ." Sandor went on.

I got up from the table and walked slowly out of the dining room and into the hall before going upstairs to my room. I heard footsteps outside just before a sharp, urgent knock on the door echoed through the still nearly empty house. When I opened the door, I saw Mr. Cranstone standing there.

"Is my daughter here?" His voice was hard and his manner abrupt.

Before I could answer, Mama came into the hall from the kitchen. Her voice came from behind me, almost matching Mr. Cranstone's in its abruptness. "She is."

I stood aside, happy to let Mama deal with the situation. She had a dab of flour on the tip of her nose, and her jaw, though not set tightly, was firm.

"Then may I have her, please?"

"Of course." Mama didn't ask him in and I was glad, for the place was bare. She walked to the dining-room door. "Debbie, your daddy is here. He wants to take you home to lunch."

There was no sound from inside the room. Debbie obviously didn't want to go. Mama went in and a few moments later came out carrying Debbie, who was crying and making it plain that she had no desire to leave. Sandor followed them, carrying his book. Mama took Debbie to her father.

"I'm afraid they were in the middle of a story. Debbie wanted to hear the end. Perhaps—"

Mr. Cranstone took Debbie from Mama. "I'd be very much obliged," he said, "if you would stop your son encouraging her here in future—"

"Debbie came—" Sandor began. Mama hushed him.

"You were saying, Mr. Cranstone?"

"I was saying— Oh, Debbie, be quiet. Please don't encourage her here in future. It's very worrying. I don't wish her—"

"Of course. Good morning." Mama closed the door, leaving Mr. Cranstone, who, from the tone of his voice, was about to say something unkind, standing on the doorstep.

It was easy to tell that Mama was hurt or angry or both. She put her arm around Sandor's shoulders and walked him back to the kitchen. He was very near tears.

"Mama, Debbie knocked on the door," he said. "I didn't—"

"Hush, darling. It doesn't matter. Don't worry your little self. Come and help me finish getting the lunch."

Poor Sandor, I thought. He doesn't understand. I told myself I would be extra kind to him to make up for it. I followed them into the kitchen.

Mama said, "I ought not to have done that. It hasn't solved any problem." Her serious look dissolved in the beginnings of a smile at the corners of her mouth. "But it gave me an awful lot of satisfaction."

The following day Mr. Slater came. He was a short, dapper man who wore glasses. He was dressed in a black jacket and pinstripe trousers; he had a thick black mustache, and his sparse black hair shone like patent leather. Mama showed him over the house, and his birdlike glance pecked at everything. His manner was brisk, he was courteous to Mama, and Brad and I quite liked him.

When he had completed his tour and was sitting in the dining room sipping a cup of coffee I had made, he said, "My word—but you have done wonders already."

Brad and I warmed to him still more.

He smiled—a wide generous smile. "Mrs. Kopchek, I think we can do business. We're two foreigners in a strange land, and we can help each other."

I didn't understand him referring to himself as a foreigner. He looked so English. It must have shown on my face, for he said, "I mean it—about the foreigners. Oh, I'm English all right, but I'm not a Chadhaven man, and I've only been here just over a year. So to the natives I'm an outsider. And you would be surprised at the amount of resistance I have come up against since I've been here."

"You mean people don't like you?" Mama asked.

"I wouldn't go so far as that. But there is certainly a resentment because I bought the hotel. I gave a higher price than that offered by some Chadhaven businessmen who got together to buy it. I have already heard the same sort of resentful talk about the council letting you take over this house."

"Yes—we haven't been exactly welcomed by our neighbors."

"The Cranstones? No, I don't suppose you would be. He's not on the council, but he's a big bug in the local chamber of commerce and the Ratepayers' Association, as well as being the prime mover in the formation of the Chadhaven Junior Sailing Club. They were hoping to rent this place for a song. Do a bit of renovation and use it as their club and headquarters."

"We know."

"Ah, well." Mr. Slater smiled again. "When we've been here about twenty years—if we can stick it that long—maybe they'll no longer consider us as foreigners. But now, let's get back to business. I have quite a bit of reasonable furniture in store and some carpeting and linen as well. If there isn't enough there, I don't mind making the outlay to buy more."

"That's wonderful." I couldn't help bursting in on the conversation.

Mr. Slater looked at me over his rather thick-lensed

glasses. "Don't think I'm doing this out of the kindness of my heart, young lady. By being able to use your rooms when my own at the hotel are full, I can count on maybe fourteen extra guests to feed and so on. I have the dining-room capacity for that. I can't enlarge my building, so using your house as an annex is the next best thing. I shall make more money—and so will you."

He took a sip of his coffee. Then he went on: "We'll value the furniture and fittings—curtains, carpets, linen, sheets, and things like that—which will completely furnish the house. Then you will, in effect, buy them off me by means of me deducting what I will have to pay you each week for the guests you take in. If we have a good summer this year, you should very nearly clear the debt in one season, and next year you should be making money. To protect us both from each other," he smiled again, "we will have an agreement drawn up by a solicitor. Agreed?"

Mama nodded happily. It really did seem a wonderful idea for furnishing the house in the first place and for a source of income later.

Mr. Slater worked fast. Within a week all the rooms—except the attic rooms, which we were not going to decorate until the roof had been repaired—had been carpeted, curtained, and furnished, as well as the stairs and hall. The agreement had been drawn up by a solicitor called Mr. Cracknell, and Mama had signed it with a flourish.

Maybe some of the carpeting and furniture were not

what we would have chosen, but the hollow emptiness was gone from the rooms, and we had armchairs to loll in. That alone, I thought—after sitting on nothing but hard upright chairs for so long—made it all worthwhile.

Mama said she felt like a queen, and she dusted and polished every stick of furniture in sight so often that Brad and I had to be very firm with her. (She was working hard at Chad Hall, and when she was home she couldn't stop herself from making the house glisten.)

Brad had arranged with Mr. Keeping, the foreman where he did his holiday work, to borrow a ladder to mend the roof and paint the upstairs windows. On the Thursday before the Monday we were due to start school, I went with him to collect it and carry it home. We chose Thursday, when Mama had to be at the Hall all day, as she was nervous about Brad going onto the roof. I was nervous for Brad too, and I believe Brad was as well. He had never climbed a tall ladder before. He gave no sign of being nervous, but his manner when the hazards of ladder climbing and roof repairing were mentioned was offhand and flippant. Knowing Brad, I knew that this was just a cover-up for the way he really felt.

But I must tell you about the way we brought the ladder home. When we arrived at Fryer's boatyard before nine o'clock in the morning, we were met by Mr. Keeping, the yard foreman, a short, stocky man who seemed as broad and thick about the chest and shoulders as he was tall. He had short, gray hair; a square, lined face; and a stubble of gray beard on his chin. He had a large mouth and wrinkles at the sides of his eyes.

" 'Ullo, young Koppechick," he said as Brad led me into the yard. "Ooh's this, then? No need to tell me—your sister, eh? 'Ullo, Miss Kopperknob." He was smiling and somehow his play on our name, tying it up with my red hair, didn't annoy me.

He went on: "I've bin thinkin'. If you're gonna mend yer roof, you'll need a roofin' ladder too. So I put one out. It's over 'ere with the other." He led us over to the yard wall, past a number of small boats in varying stages of construction, where a light metal extending ladder and a flat-looking wooden one lay at the base of the wall.

"You'll be able to manage both," said Mr. Keeping. "The big one's no 'eavier than the little 'un. Mind you don't knock out no windows when you turns into Fore Street."

The wooden roof ladder was shorter than the metal one, so we carried them lying flat, the roof ladder resting on the metal one. Brad thanked Mr. Keeping for his help, and we set off, Brad leading the way.

I was surprised at the lightness of the metal ladder, which, as the foreman had said, was no heavier than the small roof ladder.

As we turned out of the yard into the road, I called to Brad, "What's this wooden ladder for? How do you use it?"

"It's obvious. You lay it on the roof to stand on—stops you putting your feet through the tiling." Brad spoke with a superior knowledge gained from his studies of his do-it-yourself magazine.

"Then why didn't you think of it instead of Mr. Keeping?"

He turned his head and gave me a half grin. "I forgot."

I think we would have been able to get the ladders home without incident had it not been for one thing—we forgot that Thursday is market day in Chadhaven.

Brad started off a little too quickly for me, and before I stopped him I felt as if I were a slave being dragged along behind a chariot. After that, all went well until we had crossed the bridge leading to the upper end of Fore Street.

Then we were reminded with a certain amount of urgency that it was market day. Brad was halfway across the road, taking a wide turn to clear the corner of the wall, having seen that there was no traffic coming up from the lower part of the town. What we hadn't seen was a herd of cows being driven down into the town toward the market. The first indication I had was a great soulful face, surmounted by two of the longest, sharpest horns I have ever seen, staring at me reproachfully from under the ladder between me and Brad.

By the time I had screamed to Brad to stop—and he had acted on my somewhat hysterical command—I was face to face with the creature that had halted, our noses no more than an inch apart. The cow continued to look at me, more in sorrow than anger, while I stood there petrified. The animal remained under the ladder between me and Brad, looking at me as if it wanted to make sure it would know me should our paths happen to cross once more.

Brad looked around with irritation to see the cause of my screech. And then instead of coming to my rescue, he just stood there laughing his head off.

Whether the cow was suddenly taken by a sharp pain or whether it considered that we had been so close for so long that it was time for introductions to be made, I don't know. All I know is that, opening its mouth wide, the beast gave a moo to end all moos right in my face. I had always been given to understand that cows were vegetarians, but just at that minute I was willing to believe that this particular representative of the bovine race had turned man-eater—or, as it was me most closely concerned, girl-eater.

I screeched to Brad, "It's mad! It's a bull! Come and help me!"

Brad merely continued to roar his silly head off, and the cow looked me in the eye with the sorrowful expression of an elder wondering what on earth the younger generation is coming to.

Brad said—when he could speak between his idiotic bouts of laughing—"Step to one side, stupid, and walk on."

The cow gave no indication of a desire to move or even to take its hypnotic gaze off me, and to have to pass in front of that face and those horns and be forced to turn my back on the animal was more than I could have done. So I just stood there, staring in horrified fascination at the great brown-and-white eyes that blinked at me with a lazy irony from time to time.

By then it was too late for us to move, for the rest of the herd now surrounded us, passing with maddening slowness on their way to the market. I shut my eyes tight, called softly for Mama, and imagined us being tossed into the river, ladders and all, there probably to meet a damp doom in the swiftly flowing waters of the Chad.

I was vaguely aware of huge brown-and-white bodies slowly lumbering past me, behind and in front, and at one horrible moment the end of a swishing tail brushed the back of my head. Had there been no ferocious animal just an inch away, I think then that I would have climbed along the ladder to gain the somewhat doubtful safety of being near Brad.

Instead, I gave one of the best imitations of a statue that has ever been seen, said my silent farewells to Mama and Sandor, silently reproached Brad for not coming to my rescue, but forgiving him at the same time, and prepared to meet my end as bravely as I could.

I stood there and stood there, feeling like Lot's wife turned into a pillar of salt, until Brad's voice said, "You can wake up now. They've gone."

I opened my eyes slowly, not at all prepared to believe him and half expecting to see the bovine face still suspended right in front of my face. But the cows had gone—they were amiably ambling on down the street. We had by then collected quite a few amused onlookers, who had stopped to watch my interpretation of a statue.

I was so relieved to find myself still alive that I forgot to be annoyed with Brad, and we moved off, more slowly this time, so as not to become entangled in the herd of cows again.

We got home eventually, and before we started school Brad had repaired the roof and painted half the upstairs windows.

But even to this day I get a frozen feeling whenever I see a cow and there is no fence between us.

CHAPTER EIGHT

I WENT TO school warily on Monday, with mixed feelings of excitement and apprehension. At the end of the long road leading from the wrought-iron gates to the old administration building, Brad turned left to go to the boys' school and I turned right to the girls'. There were crowds of other children—boys and girls whose ages ranged from about twelve to maybe sixteen or seventeen—all doing the same as we had done. The air was noisy with the sound of their voices greeting each other at the beginning of a new term. I got quite a few curious glances. I was so obviously a new girl—and rather old to be one.

There was certainly some rule forbidding the use at assembly time of the beautifully kept playing fields that surrounded the school buildings on every side; for the girls, I noticed, kept to a large spread of tightly mown grass separated from the playing fields by an evergreen hedge. The younger ones raced around squealing and playing, while the older girls stood about in groups talking. I felt lonely and out of things, though I was satisfied with how I looked. The school dresses were very smart, and Mama herself had put the finishing touches to the alterations done by the shop. I had taken great care with my hair, and Mama and I had experimented with my straw-boater hat to see which way it looked best. I envied Brad, who merely flung his cap on the back of his head and that was that.

I was beginning to wish the bell would ring—or whatever it was they did to start school—when I saw Sheila Cranstone walking toward me. She was trying to smile, but I think my taut face made her nervous. And, anyway, she had already had a cool reception from Brad and me—on the Good Friday when we had gone on our picnic.

Since her father's unkindness about letting Debbie come to visit us, I had sworn that *never* would I have anything to do with any of the Cranstones—and that included Debbie.

"Hullo," said Sheila. "I must say our old uniform looks pretty good on you."

I tried to think of something to say that would send her right away, but when I thought of it, I couldn't put it into words. "Thank you," I said instead.

"And how in the world do you manage to make our stupid hat look attractive?"

I thought: She's being condescending. Her dress and her hat look all right on her too. So why has she got to make *that* sort of remark if she's not being condescending or trying to make fun of me? Aloud I said, "Isn't it where you're supposed to wear it—on your head?"

I looked away from her, feeling awkward, unable to bring myself to be pleasant. I felt relieved when a Senior girl appeared on the steps of the main entrance with a hand bell, which she rang lustily. The shrieking Juniors became silent, stopped their rushing about, and started to walk sedately to assigned positions and line up. The Seniors also formed lines, and I was left standing about not knowing where to go. Some mistresses made their appearance, and one of them left the main body of the school and made straight for me. I was relieved when I recognized her as Miss Fraser. I knew I was conspicuous standing alone, and I felt as if every eye was on me.

Miss Fraser smiled as she came up to me. "Hullo, Sondra. My, you look nice. Our school uniform certainly suits you."

"Hullo, Miss Fraser."

"Feel all excited?"

"Mm—sort of." I had liked Eileen Fraser when she had supervised my examination. Now I liked her even more.

"Well, come along. I'll take you to meet Miss Slant, the deputy head. Later in the morning, I expect Dr. Haisman will want to see you."

We walked slowly toward the entrance, through which most of the girls had already filed. I sneaked a glance at Miss Fraser as we walked. She looked extremely young to be a teacher, and very pretty. Her freckles suited her, and I wondered if the sun was glinting on my hair as it did on hers. I found myself thinking that I wouldn't mind wearing glasses if they looked so attractive on me. She wore a flowered dress with a three-quarter-sleeve-length bolero jacket.

"We must go into assembly first," said Miss Fraser. "You'll stand with the sixth form—I'm form mistress—and then we will go along to Miss Slant."

We walked along a wide, brightly painted corridor to the assembly hall, which spanned the girls' and boys' departments. We stood just inside the door at the back of the hall, and then with a whispered, "You will be all right here," Miss Fraser walked to the front, where she stood facing the class of sixth formers alongside whom I was standing. The hall was about equally occupied, the girls in one half, the boys in the other, with masters and mistresses standing in front facing the forms for which they were responsible. In the center stood Dr. Haisman and a portly woman of about forty in heavy horn-rimmed spectacles, wearing a severe two-piece in gray. Dr. Haisman read a prayer, a verse from a hymn was sung, and then the school broke up into its forms and left the hall.

Miss Slant turned out to be the portly woman who had been standing with Dr. Haisman. She greeted me unsmilingly when I arrived in her office.

"Good morning," she said. "You're Sondra—Kopchek, is it?"

People quite normally hesitated over our name because it is unusual, but Miss Slant's hesitation had an unpleasantness about it.

I felt my lips tighten as I answered, "Yes, Miss Slant."

"You enter the school under most exceptional circumstances. You are fifteen, aren't you? That means you have, at most, two years here."

"Mama—my mother—hoped I would be able to get the General Certificate of Education in one or two subjects in that time."

"I trust her hopes may be realized. If they're not, it won't be because of any lack of endeavor on the school's part."

"Nor on mine, Miss Slant."

The deputy head looked at me straightly for a few moments. She had rather protruding eyes, and their protuberance was emphasized by the thick-lensed glasses she wore. My answer may have sounded more pert than I meant it to and that may have been the reason for her gaze.

She went on: "You have been given an advantage which hundreds of children would envy. I trust you will do your best to show you are entitled to a place in the school." She rearranged some papers on her desk, then she said, "Very well. That is all."

The coldness of my reception at first made me want to run out of school. But this feeling soon passed when I remembered the friendliness of Miss Fraser and the kindness of Dr. Haisman.

I saw him later in the morning. He gave me a wide

smile, stood up from behind his large mahogany desk, and only sat down again when I was seated.

We spoke of my hopes in obtaining G.C.E. in English, French, mathematics—which I loathed—and geography.

"It's a lot to cram into two years," said Dr. Haisman, "but I think you stand a very good chance of doing it." He paused for a few moments and looked thoughtfully out of the French windows at one of the Junior boys' forms doing physical training. Then he turned to me, smiled, and said, "I've already seen your brother. He tells me he plays football."

"I believe he is quite good for his age."

"Fine. He must show us what he can do in the autumn. And you, Sondra—do you play any games? Tennis? Netball?"

"I've played handball."

"Mm—well, I suppose it's not much different from netball, really. I think you should try to get into one of the netball teams. All work and no play is no good to you. I'm sure Miss Fraser—your form mistress, isn't she?—will be very happy to help you. Now, just one more thing before I send you back to work. While you are here, don't ever be discouraged or disheartened. There is, as I said before, some opposition to your being given places in the school—your brother and you. The best way to kill that opposition in the school is to do well. And that I'm sure you will do. I'm sure too that you will make friends here. I hope you'll be happy. And now, my girl, back to your class. You've got a lot to get through and only a little time to do it."

I went back to class with a warm glow inside me. Dr. Haisman's words, Dr. Haisman himself with his kindness, had that effect on me, and the chill memory of Miss Slant was pushed in the background. Brad and I, exchanging notes on the way home that evening—we lunched at school but in different halls—thought that we should like the school and do well there.

Brad found the same thing that I had—friendly curiosity from most of the boys or girls with whom we came into contact. And our accent obviously amused and attracted them. Brad had come up against no equivalent to Miss Slant in the masters, but there were one or two Senior boys—Brad was in the Middle School, a class higher than his age—who were friends or hangers-on of Philip Cranstone and who eyed Brad with no welcome. I envied him his chunky sturdiness—a rocklike trait that prevented this having any effect on his spirits or determination.

As we crossed the old quayside with the chestnut trees in their new bright-green leaves and the sun gilding the grass and making the early dandelions more golden, Sandor came limping eagerly toward us from the direction of the house, waving and smiling broadly. He had arrived home some fifteen minutes before and had been waiting impatiently ever since for us to arrive so that we could tell him all about our new school.

We started to tell him and then had to begin all over

again for Mama when we arrived indoors. Mama listened as she made the tea, smiling at our enthusiasm, happy for us. And not smiling so much when Brad told her, laughing, of the Cranstone clique that had eyed him with hostility. Her smile went altogether when I told her my impression of Miss Slant, and her face became troubled. It was now that Brad's surprising sympathy and understanding, which I had noticed before, came again.

"Now, Mama," he said, the man of the family—a position he had taken very seriously since Father's death—"you mustn't worry. Sondra and I will do nothing to make things difficult. And also, above Cranstone and Miss Slant, there is Dr. Haisman."

She brightened at the mention of Dr. Haisman. "Brad, my darling—you're right. Dr. Haisman is a good man. But I wonder why it is difficult for some people to accept us?" She poured our tea as we sat around the table in our now comfortably furnished dining room. "They will—if only we show them we like *them* and don't try too hard to make them like *us*."

I thought of the way I had snubbed Sheila Cranstone and felt very mean with myself. But as I remembered how Mr. Cranstone had been with Sandor, and Philip Cranstone's insolent attitude to all of us, my heart hardened again.

Sandor cut across my thoughts. "Some boys at my school call me Gimpy Chopstick. Do you know what 'gimpy' means, Mama?"

Mama shook her head and looked helplessly at me, as

she always did when some English idiom defeated her.

"It's a friend name, perhaps?" she queried.

"A nickname, Mama," I said. "But I don't know what it means. Do you, Brad?"

He shook his head. "But I'll find out tomorrow. There's a boy I sit next to called John Peters—I like him; I think he may be a friend—I'll ask him."

We had very little homework to do that evening—just sorting out our books, putting our name, form, and address in our exercise books, and I had a chapter to read from the classic we were doing that term. We did it immediately after tea, and then Brad changed and went outside to continue painting the guttering and gutter boards and upstairs windows, while I changed into my jeans and went up to the attics to help Mama finish off the decorating of our top rooms.

Brad was now quite used to climbing the ladder, and Mama, seeing how sure he was, had ceased to worry. Sandor helped us all by running and fetching things or sitting on the bottom of Brad's homemade steps when Mama and I were working on them. If he couldn't help us, he went out and sat on the bottom rung of the ladder and talked to Brad.

Brad had now, of course, given up his afternoon job at the boatyard, but we had made an arrangement with Mrs. Poplin for Brad and me to share the newspaper route, each of us delivering on alternate mornings. We planned to share the thirty shillings, clubbing together to give Sandor his pocket money and paying for our school dinners. It eased the strain on Mama's purse. Brad had come with me on my early-morning delivery so that he would know my route, and tomorrow would be his first morning on his own.

Mama stopped working in the attic before I did to get the supper—Sandor had put himself to bed earlier—and Brad, with next morning's early work in mind, was quite happy to stop painting, although there was still some daylight left.

We went to bed that night with the feeling that we had taken another big step forward in our new life.

But the following morning a blow fell—a blow which was as unexpected as it was sinister.

Brad was off on his route, and from the kitchen came the delicious smell of breakfast being cooked by Mama. We had never had a cooked breakfast before coming to England, but Mama was so determined to become as English as possible that everything typically English was a "must." And we soon got to like and look forward to bacon and eggs.

I came downstairs just in time to see the letter-box flap open and a letter drop onto the mat. This was such a rare occasion in our house that I swooped on it excitedly. But as I picked up the envelope my excitement vanished.

The envelope was addressed to "The Kopchek Family, 'Light View,' The Quay, Chadhaven."

But the address was not written. All sorts of type had been cut from newspapers to make up the words. It looked odd, and I turned the envelope over and over in my hands, wondering what it could be. Mama came into the hall.

"A letter for us?" she called, coming toward me. In silence I handed her the envelope. She looked at the address for some moments before, with an almost angry movement, she tore the envelope open.

I stood there, watching her face, trying to read what she was feeling. Her mouth tightened and an almost hurt look came into her eyes as she read. She continued to stare down at it for some moments after she had finished reading. Then she handed it to me.

The letter was also composed of letters of differing type cut from a newspaper. It read: "To the Kopcheks. You are not wanted in Chadhaven. You are foreigners. We do not like you. We shall see that you leave. Why not go now, before you are forced? There will be trouble if you don't."

There was no signature, no sign from whom it had come. And to me it was almost as bad as the bullets that killed my father.

CHAPTER NINE

THE LETTER didn't put Brad off his breakfast as it did Mama and me. "Is there a postmark on the envelope?" he asked when he read it. Neither Mama nor I had thought of looking—we had been so mesmerized by the weirdness of the address.

Mama picked up the envelope between her finger and thumb as if it were dirty and looked at it. "Postmark . . . ? Yes . . . you can just read it—Minthampton and yesterday's date."

"So," said Brad, putting down his tea cup. "It was delivered by the postman and not by the person who composed it."

That was another point I hadn't thought of. I had taken it for granted that the letter had been delivered by the normal post services. I grasped what Brad was getting at. If it had been delivered by the person who wrote it, I had missed a fine chance of seeing who it was. But as the postman had brought it, the possibility didn't arise, and I felt relieved.

"Mama, you should take it to the police."

Mama took the letter from Brad, her face thoughtful. "Maybe—maybe it is just a joke . . . perhaps . . . No, we won't go to the police. If more come, then maybe. But we don't want to make a fuss. It would be better, I think, if we said nothing to anybody just now about it."

"It's not what I would call a good joke," I said.

"Nor I. If another comes, then I will take it to the police. But not this one—not now."

Brad said, as we walked across the quay to Fore Street, "Now who would take all the trouble of going the twenty miles to Minthampton to post that stinking letter? They really must want to get us out of the town."

"There's only one family that I know of—the Cranstones. They've shown plainly enough they want to get rid of us."

"They're the obvious answer, true," said Brad. "But surely they would realize that they would be the first ones we would suspect?"

"Maybe they're so sure they have the rest of the town—or most of it anyway—on their side that they just don't care."

"Then why go to all the trouble of going to Minthampton to post the beastly thing? Why go to the trouble of putting it together and not signing it in the first place?"

I shrugged. "I don't know. But I bet it was one of the Cranstones."

Brad said, "Well, anyway, there's not much we can do about it right away. I think maybe Mama is right. Someone may have done it for a joke."

"A horrid, beastly, stinking joke!"

"I can understand Mama not wanting to make a fuss if that is so. But if it's not a joke and we get another, then we should go to the police."

"So much for our 'new life,' " I said bitterly. And neither of us spoke again until we arrived at school.

During break, I was talking to Mary Stott, the school captain, and Sally Crewe, another prefect, who with Miss Fraser ran the netball team. They were asking me if I'd played netball, and we were arranging for me to have a trial one evening. Just then Sheila Cranstone and another girl walked slowly past. I heard Sheila say, ". . . and so Daddy took us all into Minthampton last night to see the Ice Show—it's on for a week at the Theater Royal."

I didn't hear very much of what Mary and Sally were saying after that—just that I was to turn up for a trial the following evening. For the rest, Sheila Cranstone's words kept pounding in my ears: ". . . and so Daddy took us all into Minthampton last night . . ."

Oh, I thought, they must hate us a lot. Sheila's words burned on, confirming what I had thought—that one of them had sent the letter.

At lunch Sheila Cranstone came and sat next to me in the dining hall. "Hullo," she said. "Sally Crewe tells me you're going to have a netball trial tomorrow night. I do hope you make it. We had a good team last term, but we've lost two or three of our best players. I'd love to see you on the team."

"Then why are you so keen to get rid of us—to get rid of the Kopcheks from Chadhaven?" The words were out before I could stop them.

She looked at me in amazement. "What do you mean?"

"Why did you go to the trouble of cutting letters and words out of newspapers and sticking them on notepaper, telling us to get out of Chadhaven?"

"I don't know what you're talking about."

"It was a horrible anonymous letter—the sort that people not right in the head send. And it was posted in Minthampton yesterday. And yesterday evening you and your family went to Minthampton—I heard you say so." Forgotten were Mama's instructions to say nothing about the letter to anyone. I was hot with anger. "And if you think you are going to throw suspicion from yourself by being nice in a sickly sort of way, then it won't work." I stopped, breathless, my face burning and all of me trembling with indignation and fury.

Sheila looked at me, her eyes wide, her face troubled. "You've had an anonymous letter telling you and your family to get out of Chadhaven?"

"You know very well we have, because one of you Cranstones sent it."

She continued to look at me shaking her head slowly. "You're wrong, Sondra—"

"Don't call me Sondra."

"You are wrong. We didn't send that note. We didn't write it, and we did not send it. We were together all the time in Minthampton last night and none of us went near a letter box or post office."

"Huh! Then one of you got someone else to post it for you."

For the first time I saw Sheila really angry. The soft gentle lines of her face seemed to tighten—just as I had sometimes seen Mama's tighten on the rare occasions when she was angry. A frown came to Sheila's forehead, and her lips were pursed.

"I have taken all I am going to take from you, Sondra Kopchek. I've had rows at home because I have stood up for your family against Daddy and Phil. I've tried to explain to your mother—who's a sweet—about us. I have tried to make friends with you and have been rudely snubbed for my pains. Now—get this straight. None of my family would stoop so low as to send rotten, melodramatic anonymous letters. None of us have. If Daddy wants to get rid of you Kopcheks from being next door to us—or even being in Chadhaven at all—he can do it without the help of anonymous letters, believe *me!*"

Sheila slammed down her knife and fork, and the noise made old Miss Burns, the domestic science mistress, due to retire at the end of the year, jump and drop her pince-nez in the soup tureen.

I watched Sheila walk out of the hall, feeling a little

breathless myself. Somehow I had a desolate feeling as I saw the door swing shut behind her. It was as if she had slammed the door against any possibility of our being friends. And I suddenly realized how much, deep down, I wanted to be friends with her.

It wasn't until Brad and I were more than halfway home that evening that I was able to tell him about Sheila. His friend John Peters, who lived not very far from us, walked most of the way with us. He and Brad were the same age, though John was taller and thinner, with an intelligent face and kind eyes. His talk and movements were gentle, and he wanted passionately to become a doctor. His father was a dustman. I could well understand why Brad liked him.

When he had gone I told Brad about Sheila. He said, "I think you'd be right if you believed her. But we should be warned by what she said about her father being able to get rid of us by other means." He walked along swinging the small case in which he carried his schoolbooks. "Gimpy," he said suddenly, "is a not always pleasant way of referring to someone who has a limp. John Peters says it depends on the way it's used—how it's said."

"Oh!" I hoped for Sandor's sake there was nothing unpleasant about the way it was spoken.

We had a demonstration of it not long after, when we saw, at the end of Fore Street, Sandor and an equally small but scruffy boy. The boy's socks were wrinkled around his ankles like squeezed-up concertinas. His knees were muddy, and the knot of his tie was underneath his left ear. He had a button nose and brown hair that stuck up from his head like spikes.

We heard him call, as they parted, "Cheerio, Gimpy, then—see yer termorrer."

And Sandor, with a broad smile on his face, waved good-by to his friend. Brad and I looked at each other and smiled. Here at least was one boy who made the word sound friendly and warm.

Sandor said as we came up to him, "Did you see my friend? His name's George Keeping. His father's foreman of the boatyard you worked for, Brad."

Brad grinned. "He's not overtidy, is he?"

Sandor grinned back. "No," he said, "but I like him. We all call him Chunkhead."

"You're a bit late tonight," I said.

"We played in the playground."

"Mama will be worried."

Sandor shook his head seriously. "No she won't, Sondra. I told her we had a club meeting in the playground this evening and that I would be a bit late."

"Club meeting?"

"Sure—they voted me a member yesterday. It's called the Four Star Rangers."

"It sounds all right. What does the club do?"

"Oh—play about. *You* know—marshals and badmen. And we swap stamps an' things like that. When we play Matt Dillon I've always got to be Chester, they say, because of my limp." Sandor sounded pleased and proud. It seemed he had been accepted, and his limp was being an advantage to him instead of a drawback.

When we got home, Mama had arrived only a few minutes before. She had been busy at Chad Hall, getting it ready for a meeting that was to be held that night. I helped her get the tea. And as I saw her move about, talking happily of the day's work, I hoped that when I became a woman, I would be as beautiful as she. Neither of us said anything about the letter, and I did not mention my clash with Sheila Cranstone. I felt guilty about it because Mama had said it would be better to say nothing about it to anybody.

We had tea and then did our homework, which took us much longer than on the previous nights, and when Brad made a move to carry on painting where he had left off, Mama put her foot down. "Now you have started schoolwork properly, my darling," she told him, "there will be no housework for you in the evenings. You and Sondra earn your own pocket money, and Sandor's too, and that's enough. To do more in the evenings is too much. We will do some work on the house on Saturdays maybe."

"But Mama—you work all day and in the evenings too."

Mama smiled and ruffled her fingers through Brad's thick, wiry hair, just as she used to with Father. "Maybe so. But I am different—I'm older and bigger and stronger than you!"

This wasn't quite true, and Mama knew it. The only thing that was true was that she was older than Brad. She knew she had been exaggerating again.

"Well, anyway," she said, "it's because I say so."

I told Mama about my trial for the netball team, and she was pleased. "But you'll need proper playclothes," she said, a note of alarm in her voice. "And how can we get them in time?"

"Mama, calm down. All I need is a very short skirt, and Sally Crewe is going to lend me one of hers. I have a sleeveless blouse that will do—and white crepe-soled shoes."

"But we'll make one or buy one for you right away," Mama said.

I was full of relief the following morning when no letters were delivered, and I hoped Mama's suggestion that the letter was a joke might be true.

During the lunch recess at school, Miss Fraser explained the difference in the rules between handball and netball, and all day I had the niggling feeling that I wanted to say I was sorry to Sheila. If only she had given the slightest indication of warmth, as she had previously, I would have gone to her and apologized. But she didn't, and I was too stiff-necked to make the first move.

After school about twenty-four of us made our way to the pavilion on the other side of the playing fields, where we changed from our school clothes to our netball outfit. Sheila was among the twenty-four, and after we had changed, Miss Fraser picked two teams. Sheila was on the opposite side to me.

It was soon obvious that she was a very good player. I thought I was doing all right and only infringed the rules twice in my excitement. We were five goals to two down when it happened. Sheila had been playing rings around me, and it seemed to me she was doing it deliberately—to make me look foolish. This was not the case, but at this period I was ready to take everything the wrong way.

We were under our goal, and Sally Crewe sent over a high ball to Sheila, who jumped to take it. I jumped too, and while we were in the air Sheila's elbow caught me in the chest and sent me staggering. Normally I would have taken it as an accident that only rarely occurs in netball. But it was Sheila Cranstone's elbow which had caught me—Sheila who was usually so gentle. And I thought: Oh, how she must hate me! And I hate her too!

It happened so quickly, and my reaction must have been like lightning. I recovered from my stagger, and as Sheila landed, the ball safely grasped to take her throw at goal, I pushed her in the back and sent her sprawling. She fell, hitting her head against the post—and lay still on the ground. My anger disappeared. I stared horror-stricken at what I had done. I was vaguely aware of Miss Fraser's whistle blowing furiously behind me, and then I dropped to my knees, half-blinded with tears, and took Sheila's head onto my lap. I would have given anything to recall those few seconds of time, to undo what I had done.

"Get up and leave the field, Sondra." Miss Fraser's voice came to me cold, unreal. But I could not get up. I stayed there, cradling Sheila's head and saying over and over again, "Sheila, Sheila, I never meant to do it. Oh, please, Sheila." I may have said other things besides, but I don't remember.

What I *do* remember is the way Sheila—after an eternity it seemed, though they told me afterward it was only a few seconds—opened her eyes and stared vaguely for a moment or two until her dazed wits cleared. Then she saw my tear-stained face looking down at her.

She smiled at me and said, "Sondra, I deserved that. I shouldn't have fouled you in the first place."

Miss Fraser left the rest of the trial in charge of Sally Crewe and took Sheila and me back to the pavilion, where she had a good look at the bump and bruise and the broken skin on Sheila's temple. "How do you feel?" Eileen Fraser asked her.

"My head's ringing a bit, but otherwise I feel all right."

"I think it's just a whacking great bump you've got, but we'll go to the hospital and get an X ray just to make sure."

"Please—may I come?" I asked.

"Please, Miss Fraser," said Sheila. "I'd like her to."

"Well, all right. Now—you had both better have a

shower and then we'll go. I'll go over to the school and ring for a taxi."

In the taxi none of us spoke, though Sheila and I smiled at each other once or twice. Miss Fraser looked out of the window most of the time, and I was sad to think I was so obviously in her bad books.

We went into the Casualty Department and Sheila was taken away for her X ray.

I sat there glumly. If anything was wrong, I would never forgive myself.

Miss Fraser said, "Whatever made you do it?"

I shook my head, near tears again.

"Look, Sondra, while I've got the opportunity I want to talk to you."

I continued looking straight ahead. Nothing Miss Fraser had to say could make me feel worse than I already did.

"You've had a bitterly unhappy time—I know that. And now your mother, who must be a rather wonderful person, has brought you to England to start a new life. Some of us here want desperately for you to have that new life—and be happy. There are others who resent you being here. I know that too, for Dr. Haisman has spoken to me about it. But in the short time I've known you and have seen you at school, you give me the impression—even allowing for the newness of it all to you—that *you* resent everybody. Those who want to welcome you, as well as those who don't."

I hadn't realized how much I had allowed Philip Cranstone and his father to influence *my* attitude about pretty nearly everything else.

"You withdraw yourself from people who try to make friends."

"I wanted to play netball. That's not withdrawing myself."

"Yes, but did you join in because you wanted to make friends—or because you wanted to show off? You're a pretty good player, you know, and it seemed to me that you went out of your way to make some of the slower players look silly."

I recalled the number of inward smirks I had had during the game when I had beaten some of the girls for the ball.

"I'm being very clumsy about it, I know. But do you see what I'm trying to get at? I think you, personally, came to this country with the idea at the back of your mind that you were owed a living by all of us here for what you had been through. Instead of thinking, 'These new people and I have got to meet each other halfway—it's not got to be *all* on one side or the other.' You've got into a way of feeling sorry for yourself."

How well Miss Fraser had read me! As she spoke it seemed that her words mirrored the way I had been feeling.

"I know we have some people here who, for their own narrow reasons, don't want to see outsiders come and take things they feel should have been theirs or their friends'. Equally, there are others who really want to see you happy. Sondra, it's up to you and the way you act which side wins. *Do* you see that?"

I nodded—not thoughtlessly, for her words struck me. "I never wanted to push Sheila," I said. "Far less hurt her. You see, deep down I wanted to be friends with her. And about the other—what you've been talking about—I know what you mean. I understand."

Miss Fraser smiled at me and squeezed my arm. "Good, Sondra Kopchek. I'm glad. For you've got an awful lot about you that's nice. And I'm one of those people who want to see you and your family happy."

Sheila came back after a while with the nurse, and both of them were smiling.

"Doctor says all is well," said the nurse. "The girl's got a skull as thick as an elephant's. He's given her a sedative to get rid of the ringing bells."

Sometimes you can't describe a feeling of happiness and relief that suddenly comes to you. This was one of those times.

Miss Fraser said, "Do you feel all right to walk home, Sheila?"

"I feel fine."

"All right then, you two. I'll go on back to school and collect my bubble car and get off home. See you in the morning."

Sheila and I walked home together. We didn't say much. We both knew how I felt about what I had done —and we both knew Sheila hadn't deliberately fouled me. We both knew too that our friendship would have no effect on the way Mr. Cranstone and Philip felt.

That night, sometime after we were all in bed, I went to Mama's room and, in the darkness and softness of the night, sitting on the edge of her bed, I told her everything that had happened.

When I had finished, she hugged me and said, "Sondra, you have won us a victory—though you went about it all the wrong way and didn't deserve to."

CHAPTER TEN

THIS WAS the turning point for me. And I never again let that feeling of being sorry for myself grow so big that it drowned everything else. Whatever happened, I realized, I had Mama's love and Brad's and Sandor's, and there were others who cared too.

The following day Miss Slant saw the swelling on Sheila's temple, which had been covered with a medicated dressing, and somehow she discovered the truth of how it had happened. She sent for me and told me in a cold voice that, under the circumstances and because of my display of a temper that I was apparently unable to control, I would not be considered for the netball team, for this term at any rate. It was a great blow to me, but I didn't react as I would have a few days previously. I accepted it as a just punishment instead of thinking of it as a persecution. I had done something that might have caused Sheila much more harm than it had. My only punishment so far had been my own feelings. Now I had been punished so that others could see.

I learned later from Miss Fraser that both Sheila and Sally Crewe had pleaded with Miss Slant to cancel or at least reduce the period of my banishment from the team but that the assistant head had remained firm.

Mama was disappointed for me but said, "You can't complain, Sondra, my love. It was very wrong what you did, and it is right that you should be punished."

Two weeks went by in which Brad finished the outside painting and Mama and I completed the decoration of the top-floor bedrooms. Mr. Slater sent the furniture for them, and I was staggered at the amount of money he and Mama agreed was a fair price. But Mama said, "It is a lot of money, but already Mr. Slater has filled our spare rooms for the last week in July and the first week in August."

Brad said, "If Sandor moved in with me for the summer that would free another room."

"Wouldn't you mind, Brad?" Mama was pleased at his suggestion. "And would you be willing, Sandor?"

"I wouldn't mind at all, Mama," said Sandor. "So long as Brad doesn't make a row when he comes up to bed. He chucks his shoes down when he takes them off. I hear him sometimes."

"And if you whistle that horrible, tuneless noise like you do in your own room while you're dressing in the morning, I'll beat you over the head," retorted Brad.

"So nice we can come to a friendly arrangement," Mama said sweetly. "And if I hear either of you dropping shoes or whistling, I'll take my hairbrush to the pair of you."

Brad said, "Why did I open my big mouth?"

"I'll help you in with my bed tonight, Brad," Sandor offered.

"Good grief, I'm not going to put up with you *all* the year round. When school lets out for summer holidays will be soon enough, won't it, Mama?"

"If I am not to lose one of you in one way or another," said Mama thoughtfully, "it will be quite soon enough."

The following morning we received the second letter. This time we took it in without suspicion, for the address on the envelope was typewritten and inscribed to "Mrs. S. Kopchek."

The letter itself merely said: "You are still in Chadhaven, then? Why don't you take your family and get out while you can, before something happens?"

The postmark said the letter had been posted in Chadhaven the evening before. The envelope and the paper were cheap—the sort that could be bought anywhere.

"Take it, and the other one, to the police, Mama," I said.

"It seems I must," Mama answered unhappily.

Brad and I didn't talk much on the way to school. We had both hoped that the first letter was a short-lived joke and that there would be no more. We had wanted to believe it, and because of that we had made ourselves believe it.

Finally I said, "Brad—if it isn't a joke—what could they do to make us leave?"

"In England? Nothing, I'd say."

"But couldn't people ignore us? What if the shops refused to serve us?"

"I don't think anything like that is likely. Don't forget that we have people who like us—Dr. Haisman, your Miss Fraser, even Sheila Cranstone."

"And there's Mr. Keeping, the foreman at Fryer's—and your friend John Peters and Sally Crewe and Mary Stott. And Mrs. Poplin can't dislike us . . ." I stopped.

Brad smiled a little wryly. "And there's Mr. Slater. That makes nine people that we know of who don't mind us being here and living in 'Light View.' It's not many, is it? Out of a town of thirty thousand."

"But what about the people on the council who let Mama have the house in the first place?"

"Mm, that must make it a few more."

"But it's not knowing *who* sends those beastly letters or how many feel like that—if it's not a joke—that makes it so awful."

Halfway through the morning, Miss Slant sent for me, and I went along to her room, going over in my mind what I had done wrong. There was nothing I could think of.

When I knocked and went in she kept me standing in front of her desk for nearly five minutes while she continued writing. Finally she laid her pen down deliberately and looked up at me through her thick-lensed glasses, out of her cold, protruding eyes.

"It has been brought to my notice," she said, talking to me impersonally, "that you deliver newspapers in the mornings before school. Is that so?"

"Yes, Miss Slant."

"You actually deliver newspapers? A *girl* delivering newspapers?"

"Yes."

"You wear your school uniform and school hat, I presume?"

"Why—yes."

"I have never heard anything like it. A King Edward Grammar School girl delivering newspapers. And in school uniform, so that everybody who sees you can identify the school."

"But . . . but . . ." My voice trailed away. I couldn't understand why delivering newspapers while I was wearing my school uniform should be wrong.

Miss Slant's mouth turned down slightly at the corners. "A school such as this has certain standards which it must maintain. But I suppose it's ridiculous of me to think that you, being foreign, would understand that. By doing such a menial task you lower the dignity of the school. Do you understand that?"

"But there are things Mama—my mother—can't afford for us, and the money I get helps."

"Your mother should have thought of that before committing herself to the expense of sending you here.

But I believe you have been given a free scholarship here?"

There was unnecessary emphasis on the words "given" and "free."

"Yes, Miss Slant."

"Then I would say there seems to be little necessity for you to deliver *newspapers* for what must be a quite paltry sum."

"It isn't paltry to us."

Miss Slant looked at me almost gloatingly, and it suddenly occurred to me that she was trying to goad me into losing my temper and being downright rude to her.

"Do I detect a note of insolence in your voice?"

"I didn't mean it to sound insolent. The money my brother and I earn isn't a paltry sum to us."

"Ah—so your brother delivers newspapers too?"

"We deliver them on alternate days."

"Mm, well, I'm not interested in the petty arrangements you have made to carry out a task that is worthy only of a street-corner urchin. I want you to understand plainly that the delivery of newspapers—despite the deplorable slackening of standards in this modern day and age—does nothing but undermine the dignity of the school. I want from you an immediate understanding that you will discontinue to deliver newspapers forthwith."

"I—I'm afraid I can't do that."

Miss Slant rose from her chair, almost thrusting her

portly figure across the desk at me. "You mean you will not give me your word?"

"I—I can't. The money helps my mother. My brother and I get our pocket money and school lunch money from it."

"Very well. You force me to take the matter further. You may go."

"Miss Slant—" I wanted desperately to explain to her how important it was to us.

"I said you may go."

I turned abruptly, roused to the point where I felt like picking up the nearest object and flinging it at her. I shut the door behind me, trying not to slam it, but not entirely succeeding.

At lunch I was quiet and unhappy.

Sheila asked, "What's up, Sondra?"

I told her what had happened and she exploded.

"What! In this day and age? I've got a cousin who's at Oxford, and in the summer vacation he works as a porter on the railway to make some money to help him through. Ever so many undergraduates do it. Work in the summer, I mean. All sorts of jobs—laborers, kitchen hands, and so on. I know. He's told me. Old Slant's being a real beast."

"What did she mean by 'taking it further'?"

"I don't know. What with one thing and another, she seems to have it in for you. But try not to worry, Sondra, there are those of us who'll stand by you, believe me."

I told Brad as we walked home. Sheila walked with us, pushing her cycle. Brad said, "Surely she can't dictate what you do out of school hours? If she can, then we might just as well have stayed where we were."

Sheila said, "I'd say she has no right, but for some unaccountable reason she doesn't like Sondra, and I believe she's trying to take it out on her. Trying to frighten her. After all, I know we're a good school, and an old one, and it's a good thing to go to it. But it's never been one of those terribly toffee-nosed affairs."

"Toffee-nosed?" This was a new idiom to me.

Sheila smiled. "Well—I mean snobby. You know—all front and no back. Some people with lots of money send their children to them, believing that the more money they pay, the better the education their children will get. It doesn't always follow."

"Anyway," I said, "I'm not going to give it up. What's wrong in trying to earn money. It's better than stealing, surely, or borrowing and not being able to pay it back—or not bothering."

"Of course it is, but people like Miss Slant don't see it that way."

We walked on quietly for a while, then suddenly I said, "Brad, I'm not going to say anything to Mama about this."

"Oh, I don't know. She'd rather hear about it from you than learn of it from somebody else—as she might well."

Almost eagerly Sheila said, "Sondra, I think you

should tell her. Keeping secrets—it's well . . . Those sort of secrets . . . Even if it is to keep her from worrying . . ."

I looked at her. "I know what you mean, Sheila. You're keeping it a secret from your father and brother about being friendly with us. It's difficult and uncomfortable."

"It's only because now isn't the right time for them to know."

"But someone's bound to see you with us sometime—now, for example—and tell them. You know how things get out."

Sheila shrugged. "If that happens, then things have got to come out into the open before I'm ready for them, that's all. But one secret's enough. I think Brad's right. Your mother wouldn't thank you for not telling her."

I had been surprised at the almost immediate acceptance of Sheila by Brad when I had told him of our friendship. After all, he had been the one to make that rude move that Good Friday we had been on the picnic. Even then, though, I think that Brad, although he was two years younger than Sheila, admired her against his will and, like me, secretly longed to be friends with her. Like me, too, he had tried desperately not to admit this to himself.

Sheila rode home shortly after this, and when we got indoors and were having tea, with the shrill voices of Sandor and young George Keeping making a background descant as they played in the garden, I told

Mama about Miss Slant and my newspaper route and what I intended to do.

Mama said, "If it's a rule of the school, then you have an obligation to obey it. On the other hand, you also have an obligation to Mrs. Poplin. You just couldn't stop immediately, without giving her a chance to find someone to take your place."

"No one's said anything to me," said Brad. "I could take it over every day."

"If the rule—if there is one—applies to Sondra, it also applies to you, Brad."

"We don't know that there *is* any such rule. Sheila thinks it's just because Miss Slant doesn't like me. Mama, let's wait and see what happens? Brad and I will go on as before until something else is said."

"Maybe I should see Dr. Haisman." There was doubt in Mama's voice.

"Please, Mama, no. Let me work this out for myself."

"You might be made to leave."

"Well, I'm fifteen, anyway—"

Mama looked at me for a few moments, then she smiled. "So. But if I have to be told anything, don't leave it until it's too late, eh?"

Brad said, "Mama, what did the police say—about the letter?"

Mama didn't answer immediately. Then after a while she looked up and said, "I haven't told them. I feel—I feel it would be better for us if we could weather this storm on our own. Without making a fuss. I—oh—it's difficult to explain. But we're new here, and—well, I just feel we should try and fight our own battles. If it gets too big for us, then—"

"I think you're wrong, Mama, but—like you said to Sondra—if the police have to be told, don't let us leave it until it's too late."

Mama told the police the following day—we had received the third letter, which read: "Kopcheks—get out! You are occupying a house to which you have no right. You have two places in the grammar school, and you have no right to those either. Get out before one of you gets hurt."

Mama went to the police because of this—and because when we went out of the house to go to school, we saw that mud had been flung on the walls of the house. Mud from the marsh. And in this same mud, words had been scrawled over the brickwork—words which said: "Kopcheks—get out!"

We stood looking at the filth, our hearts thudding. Her face pale, but squared and angry, Mama said, "Now they're attacking our castle, my darlings. They're attacking the Kopcheks' castle!"

CHAPTER ELEVEN

THIS WAS the period in which things moved so swiftly that I still confuse the days and weeks when they happened. After we received the third letter, Mama missed work to go to the police. Instead of staying at school for lunch, Brad and I went home to start cleaning the mud off the walls, only to find that the police, under their Inspector's orders, had already done so.

I was amazed and so was Brad. "The *police* cleaned it for us?"

Mama smiled a little sadly. "Yes, Brad. We're not in our old country, remember?"

"The daubing and the mud writing on our walls made me forget, Mama."

"What do they say—the police?" I asked.

"What *can* they say, yet? They've taken the letters, and they've taken plaster casts of some of the footprints in the flower bed near the wall. They were kind and told me not to worry. A reporter and a photographer from the local paper came, but the police didn't let them worry me. I don't know if the photographer took any pictures. Now I must hurry—I've got to catch up with my work at the Hall."

Brad said, "Have you had any lunch, Mama?"

"No, but—"

"I'll get us all something," I said, "and make a cup of tea. You must have something." I went into the kitchen before she could argue.

We walked part of the way to the Hall with Mama, then we went on to school. Before we left her, Mama said, "Don't worry about this thing, my sweethearts. Listen to me—a place where the police will clean away filth when it's not part of their job, and when they don't have to, is not a bad place. Remember what those policemen did for us—and then say to yourselves, 'There can't be much wrong with a place like that.' "

Mama had told us she might not be back until sometime after we arrived home from school. This had happened quite often before, and on these occasions I got the tea ready for the boys. We were somewhat surprised, therefore, to find Mama already at home when we arrived.

She had that air of busy determination about her that Father had loved so much. It only came to Mama when something rather important was afoot—something about which she was not entirely at ease.

Brad and I looked at each other, knowing the signs and wondering. She greeted us as she always did, with an almost eager happiness.

We had tea, and Sandor scrambled down from the table to go to the gate to wait for little Chunkhead Keeping, who was coming to play in the garden.

Then Mama said, "Mr. Slater came to see me at the Hall this afternoon."

"Oh!" Had he thought better of his bargain with Mama? I got up from the table, walked to the window, and looked out. I saw Sheila on her cycle shoot out of the gate next door and go pedaling away along the quay. I turned to Mama questioningly.

Mama raised an eyebrow and half smiled. "There's a group of people in the town called the Ratepayers' Association. They try to keep the town council from wasting the money they pay in rates. And to hear Mr. Slater talk, they fight a losing battle all the time. Well, anyway, tonight they have a meeting at Chad Hall. I have been getting the place ready for them."

Brad shifted in his chair, wishing Mama would come to the point.

"Mr. Slater is a member of the Ratepayers' Association, and he had a letter telling him about the meeting and why it had been called. So he came to tell me."

"But why, Mama?"

"Because, my fine Bradislav Kopchek, the two main things they are going to discuss are why the housing committee of the council let *us* have this house—when they had previously turned down local plans and requests for it—and why should two foreign children be given two of the four free places in the grammar school, preventing local children from having them?"

"Ah! So it isn't only the letter writer and the Cranstones and Sondra's fat Miss Slant we have against us."

Mama nodded. "It seems not. And Mr. Cranstone is to be chairman of the meeting. And they are going to discuss ways and means of making the council go back on their agreement with us over the house."

"But what can they do about Brad and me being at the grammar school? Dr. Haisman said he had the last word on that."

"That's true. But some governors of the school are also town councilors, and two are members of the Ratepayers' Association. I don't know—but they might be able to force Dr. Haisman to do something about it."

"Oh, Mama—what can we do? Against so many people?"

"*I* am going to the meeting and see what they have to say. And then *I* may have something to say too."

"But how can you?"

"Why not? Don't I pay rates? Don't that—I mean, *doesn't* that make me a ratepayer? With a perfect right to attend the meeting? And, anyway," added Mama with a simple sort of logic, "if they shut the doors and won't let me in, I have a key to the back entrance."

Now the reason for Mama's busy determination was clear. She rose from the table. "The meeting starts at half-past seven. I am going to change. And then I'm going to the Hall."

Brad said as she left the room, "Mama, you'll be the best-dressed and prettiest caretaker there ever was."

Mama turned her head in the doorway. "*That* was the general intention," she said.

I don't suppose for one minute that we had any right to attend the meeting—Brad and I—and at first our idea was merely to walk with Mama to the Hall. But Mama had timed her entrance well—right on time, when the Hall was buzzing with conversation and nobody was paying much attention to people coming in. After Mama had disappeared inside, there must have been one of those flashes of silent messages between Brad and me, for we suddenly looked at one another, turned, walked up the steps to the entrance, and crept unobtrusively into the meeting. We sat at the back behind a pillar, where we could neither see much nor be seen by anyone else. We could see a portion of the platform, where, behind a table, sat Mr. Cranstone, flanked on one side by a man I didn't know. Our position behind the pillar prevented us from seeing farther than Mr. Cranstone's right elbow. We kept the pillar between us and the entrance in case someone coming in should spot us and have us ejected or something. We couldn't see Mama—all we could see was a narrow wedge of heads, back view, opening out and becoming fairly wide at the platform. The Hall wasn't full, but the voices seemed to go on and on, louder and louder. We wondered if the meeting was ever going to start. But eventually, by Brad's wristwatch—which had been Father's—it got underway fifteen minutes late.

One or two items of business were dealt with that had nothing to do with us, and during this time we tried to see where Mama was sitting, but we still couldn't find her. And then Mr. Cranstone rose.

"Now," he said, "we come to the two main items on the agenda. The property known as 'Light View' and the method of allocating scholarships at the King Edward Grammar School. I think you all know the history of 'Light View,' but I will briefly outline the position for those of you who are not in possession of all the facts. 'Light View' was originally owned by Mr. Francis Streeter, but during the war it was requisitioned by the Royal Navy, who used Chadhaven and its unique facilities to train personnel—Royal Marine Commandos. At the end of the war, the town council took over the requisition as a temporary measure to assist them in overcoming the acute housing shortage. Indeed, for a while, I believe it housed two families, but it was soon empty again and remained so for a considerable time. During this time, the council bought the property from the owner. On various occasions, public bodies in the town applied to the council either to rent or purchase the property.

"The Rotary Club wanted to turn it into a holiday home for children from the industrial Midlands and the North, and a group of businessmen sought to develop the site as a hotel. And there were other applications too. But during that period, the council were toying with the idea of developing the whole of the strip from the mouth of the river up to Heron Creek as a foreshore, to make an additional attraction for visitors. Consequently all applications were turned down.

"Later the council had some crackbrained idea of renovating 'Light View' and turning it into a civic community center. But this came to nothing in the face of opposition."

I could imagine from where the strongest opposition came—Frank Cranstone wouldn't want a community center, of all things, right next door to *his* home.

He went on: "With the formation of the Chadhaven Junior Sailing Club, it became necessary to find headquarters for the club. By this time the council, which had been dithering with one idea after another over the development of the foreshore, had finally decided they could not improve on nature and decided to leave everything as it was.

"But when the Junior Sailing Club applied to purchase the property—which was fast becoming derelict—it was met yet again with a flat refusal. And then, before we know where we are, the property is sold to a foreign family. Not—and this is the important part—with the approval of the full council sitting in open session, but by the housing committee, who decided on this inexplicable move while sitting in secret session in committee.

"I feel—and I know a number of the members of the Ratepayers' Association feel as I do—that the committee had no right to dispose of the property without the consent of the full council. In short, that what they have done is illegal and that the council, in the interests of Chadhaven, have but one course—to inform the present occupiers that unfortunately the contract is illegal, that they are not the true owners of 'Light View.' What money was paid for the property must be returned to them, and they must be instructed to vacate it as soon as possible.

"We have with us tonight"—Mr. Cranstone looked down at the man on his left—"Mr. Fenner, who is one of the Ratepayers' representatives on the council, and he has been most outspoken in the council chamber against this typically woolly-headed decision of the people who are supposed to look after the interests of the people of Chadhaven.

"It is all very well for the council to treat this foreign family as unfortunate people who have suffered in the cause of freedom—I've no doubt that they have. But surely the interests of our own townsfolk come before those of outsiders who have contributed nothing to the well-being of Chadhaven in the past and are not likely to in the future? The prosperity of us all in Chadhaven is bound up in the small boatbuilding industry. So that the town's prosperity may continue, it is vital that our young people are attracted to stay in Chadhaven and not seek their fortunes in larger towns elsewhere. Owing to the lack of foresight of the town council over the years, we are extremely badly off for amenities for our young folk, who have in ever-increasing numbers sought their amusement and livelihood in the larger towns not so far away.

"It was with the idea of helping to stop this drift that the Junior Sailing Club was formed. But the council, by depriving the club of the only suitable headquarters available, have done their best to kill the idea.

"It is time that the Chadhaven council stopped trying to be philanthropists to unknown strangers and looked to the people who have made our town what it is today—a small, close-knit, and, at the moment, thriving community. It is our duty as the responsible citizens of the borough to make the council see that they have acted wrongly in this matter and force them to put the matter right."

Mr. Cranstone sat down and was applauded. Mr. Fenner had his say, repeating much of what Mr. Cranstone had said. Then other people in the Hall stood up and spoke. But it seemed that Sheila's father had said it all, for none of them put anything new before the meeting, and no one spoke in favor of us being allowed to keep possession of "Light View."

"Lot of old windbags," Brad whispered. "They clack on and on like a lot of old hens."

When everybody seemed to have had enough of emphasizing what everybody else had already said, Mr. Cranstone, having taken a long drink of water, stood up again.

"Oh, golly," whispered Brad again, "how he does go on—and on—and on."

"The other question in which we as ratepayers should have a much larger say is in the allocation of free and assisted scholarships to the grammar school." Mr. Cranstone was well in his stride once more and appearing to enjoy the sound of his own voice. "Although the King Edward does not come under the local education authority, it is the people of Chadhaven who have kept the school in being by sending their sons and daughters there. And the fees we pay are quite substantial. That is why I—and many others with me—believe that the ratepayers should have a say in the allocation of free and assisted scholarships. At the moment, it is a privilege we do not possess. This matter has recently been brought to a head by the allocation of two free scholarships to two foreign children. I understand the children were set a test long after the regular entrance examination had been held and, on the result of that test, were given two free places, over and above the heads of local children. Now, this is a specific case of hardship being forced on our own townspeople so that outsiders—and foreigners at that—might benefit. Two local children who had earned those places by right of passing the regular entrance examination were put down the very limited list and were not accepted into the school.

"Having passed the exam which entitled them to at least an assisted scholarship, their parents now find that, because the headmaster sees fit, two foreign children get the places, and the local children can't have the benefit of the education they deserve, because their parents can't afford the fees in the ordinary way. I can only describe the whole affair as shady."

There was a slight crackle of hand clapping and a rustle of movement in the Hall. And we saw Miss Slant rise to her feet, her portly figure square and aggressive.

"Mr. Chairman," she said, and turned her head this way and that, embracing the whole of the audience in her glance. The electric lights were reflected in the circles of her thick-lensed glasses like shafts of glittering vengeance.

"Mr. Chairman," she went on, "I have direct knowledge of this business—which you have rightly described as shady—and with your permission I . . ."

I didn't hear the rest of what Miss Slant was saying. I couldn't believe that anyone could be so disloyal. I felt that no matter what Miss Slant's opinions on the situation were, this was no place to air her views or disclose any knowledge that she might have because of her position. It was a stab in the back for Dr. Haisman.

From the tone of her voice it appeared to me that Miss Slant had risen on the spur of the moment, because she could no longer contain herself. Her feelings—vented apparently only on me so far—had to find wider expression, it seemed.

These thoughts went through my mind so strongly that I was aware only of the sound of her voice, not the words she spoke.

And then suddenly her voice was drowned out by the chanting of about a dozen voices from the back of the Hall, near the entrance:

K—O—P—C—H—E—K

KOPCHEK!

HOORAY!

The words, repeated over and over again, produced immediately an almost audible swivel of heads, followed by a numbed silence from the audience.

Brad and I almost jumped from behind our protective pillar to see what was happening.

Led by Sheila Cranstone, some eight or nine girls of my form—Sally Crewe and Mary Stott included—were standing in a group throwing their voices defiantly at the heavy, open-mouthed figure standing in the audience.

CHAPTER TWELVE

IT WAS THEN that I felt I belonged to Chadhaven. Sheila and the girls had learned somehow of the meeting and had come to stand by us. A delighted grin spread over Brad's face. I grabbed his hand and, pulling him with me, ran to join the chanters. I stood next to Sheila and lifted my voice with the others:

K—O—P—C—H—E—K

KOPCHEK!

And then the cheers. It was a noise to stop the flow of words from the meeting.

Sheila noticed me, and the tense expression on her face gave way to a quick smile.

After that I was only vaguely aware of what happened. Mr. Cranstone, his face pale with what I suspect was a mixture of humiliation and anger, jumped up. "How dare you!" he shouted.

The chant changed to boos—boos led by his own daughter.

Mama suddenly rose in agitation from a position near the back on the other side of the Hall. She looked toward us.

I waved to her. The chanting continued:

K—O—P—C—H—E—K

KOPCHEK!

Mr. Cranstone shouted, "Get them out of here!"

His daughter shouted back, "Try and move us!"

I had an uneasy, delicious sense of us having burned our boats.

Frank Cranstone's shout unlocked the numbed minds of the audience. Some men and women rose and started coming toward us.

"Get out, you young hooligans!"

"Call the police!"

"Disgraceful!"

"Try and get us out," we shouted.

Then suddenly another voice, firm and loud, cut through the tangled mass of words cluttering the Hall.

"It's not surprising that a meeting such as this should have brought such a violent response."

Our voices dissolved into silence.

It was Dr. Haisman, his tall figure dominating all the others in the Hall. He looked severe, determined. And his calm statement stopped the people who had been moving toward us. He looked over them, directly at us.

"You girls have had your say—ill-chosen and illegal

though the words may have been. Now leave the Hall at once. Now!"

There was no threat in his voice. No enmity either. Just a firmness that overrode everything else. Not entirely displeased, though aware that what we had done was wrong, we broke ranks slowly and left the Hall.

When we got outside, I wept and tried to embrace all the girls. They huddled to Sheila and me, responding to my feelings. Brad was on the verge of tears and felt sheepish.

"Don't worry, Sondra."

"We're with you, sweetie pie."

"They can't do anything."

All I could say through my tears was, "Thank you, thank you."

After that, Sheila, Brad, and I walked home, Sheila pushing her cycle. We were silent for most of the way, then I said, "Oh, Sheila—your father—you shouldn't."

"Why not?" she said hotly. "Oh—I love Daddy—don't think I don't. But he's so wrong! I saw the agenda for the meeting and his notes when I got home from school. I had to do something—so I went and collected the girls. And when we arrived—and heard Miss Slant . . . It just came—the chanting. . . . I had to try and do *something* to show Daddy he's wrong, and that was all I could think of."

Brad said, his voice gentle, "I'm sorry you've quarreled with your father because of us, Sheila."

She looked at Brad, a wry smile on her lips. "I've not

quarreled with him because of you, Brad—but because of *him.*"

It was an hour and a half later—we had just managed to persuade Sandor to go to bed—when we heard the crunch of car tires on the gravel. It was Mama and Dr. Haisman. He had given her a lift home from the meeting. Brad and I were a little uneasy about the arrival of Dr. Haisman, although we were prepared to defend our actions and those of the girls.

Their good humor surprised us. What surprised us even more was the fact that neither of them mentioned our presence, nor that of the girls, at the meeting.

Mama took off her hat and coat. "I'll make some coffee," she said cheerfully. "Perhaps you would like a sandwich?"

"I'd love it," answered Dr. Haisman.

Somehow we all gravitated to the kitchen, Mama and Dr. Haisman taking their high spirits with them. Mama moved about preparing the coffee and sandwiches, and I helped her in a bemused sort of way, longing to know the reason for their good humor, but not daring to ask. Dr. Haisman sat on the edge of the table, swinging one leg and watching Mama move about. She smiled and sometimes laughed softly at what he said, though I can't remember what their conversation was about. He seemed perfectly at home, and it seemed so natural for him to be in our house.

"Well," he said finally, after Mama had handed him

a cup of coffee, "our friend Cranstone's meeting hasn't done his cause much good. I don't think he expected the opposition he got. What with your friend Mr. Slater and one or two others who were swayed away from Mr. Cranstone, one might almost be inclined to think the chairman of the Ratepayers' Association suffered a severe defeat."

Mama said, "Mr. Slater and the others followed you. You were the one who defeated Mr. Cranstone. I only hope you haven't jeopardized your position by your defense of us."

Dr. Haisman smiled. "My dear lady, I don't think you need bother yourself on that score. There are seven governors of the school. Three of them might possibly try to make trouble for me. But the other four, who have no vested interest in Chadhaven, would be with me one hundred per cent."

Mama asked, "It is true, what you said about those two children?"

Dr. Haisman took a sip of coffee. Then he said, "Of course. A high standard is demanded of the children who sit for the scholarship places. There are eight places available, but it doesn't necessarily follow that those eight scholarships are awarded each year. If the standard isn't reached, the scholarships are not awarded. That is what happened last year—only five of the eight places were taken. So there were three places available, and Sondra and Brad won two of them."

"Then however did Mr. Cranstone get hold of the

idea that Brad and Sondra had pushed two local children out?" Mama's eyes were wide.

Dr. Haisman shrugged. "How *do* these stupid rumors start?"

Mama smiled happily. "I could feel the atmosphere of the place change as you spoke," she said. "It was wonderful."

"The truth always has a sort of disinfecting action. It wipes away a lot of festering rumors. I think you can be sure now that opposition to Brad and Sondra being at the school is practically dead."

It seemed almost too good to be true—but there was still so much that had been left unsaid.

"Mama . . . ?" I began.

"And Miss Slant, I feel," went on Dr. Haisman, "had the shock of her life when she saw me rise from behind the pillar. She certainly didn't expect me to be at the meeting." He sipped his coffee again. "I'm a little disappointed in Miss Slant. She's insulted my intelligence in believing that I was not aware of her feelings on this matter. Surely she couldn't think I have been blind to the fact that I have not had her loyalty for some time?" He made a small movement with his hand. "Oh, not only in this, but in other matters connected with the running of the school. Miss Slant and I don't see eye to eye on a number of things. Tonight has merely brought the matter to a head. Though I must admit," he added, "I didn't expect such action from her. And yet," he went on reflectively, "as she *has* taken such action, I ought not to be surprised, I suppose."

"Ah? So?"

"You see, of those scholarships which weren't awarded, Miss Slant had expected two of them to go to two young cousins of hers."

"But why should she expect that?"

"Because she had coached them specially, as I understand it. She spent hours, over a long period, giving them extra instruction. But when the boy and girl sat the exam, they failed. Not *just* failed, but badly."

"Oh," said Mama.

"What made it worse was that she was so certain they'd pass, she bought school uniforms for them before the results were known."

Mama drew her breath in sharply. "Such a challenge to fate to do such a thing!" she said. "Such faith—to be destroyed so completely."

"Surely it was an arrogant sort of faith?" said Dr. Haisman, a gentle smile touching his lips.

"But faith, to be good, must be strong, no?"

I looked at Mama and remembered her faith in Brad and me.

Dr. Haisman answered, "Indeed yes. But I rather fancy Miss Slant's faith was more in her own ability to teach than in the two children to learn. So that when they failed—*she* failed. It was a terrible blow to her pride. I think I can understand why she acted as she did tonight . . . and feel a certain amount of sympathy for her."

Mama's eyes glowed. "Yes?" she said. "Then I'm glad my children are at your school. And me . . . I . . . ?" Mama looked at me, a question in her eyes. I nodded, and she went on, "I too can feel sorry for Miss Slant. . . . To be so hurt . . . to be so disloyal . . . But, there, she had no chance to say whatever she had in mind to say anyway."

Dr. Haisman suddenly looked at Brad and me. "You two," he said, "had better regard yourselves as not having heard any of my remarks where they referred to Miss Slant."

"The situation with Miss Slant is going to be difficult for you," said Mama to Dr. Haisman. "But there—we mustn't talk further about that."

"True. The big thing—what it all boils down to—is that the ratepayers refused to press the council to take any action over the house and will have nothing to do with trying to influence the governors to take action over my decision about the entries to the school. All Cranstone can do now is act in his private capacity—which, without an organization to back him, takes all the sting out of the tail."

Now it was plain why Mama and Dr. Haisman were in such good spirits. And there may have been another reason too. But nobody—not even Mama or Dr. Haisman—was aware of it then.

Dr. Haisman put down his cup and looked at Mama.

"About Frank Cranstone," he said. "I've known him a long time, and I know he isn't—deep down—the harsh, narrow man he appears to be. You probably know from Sheila of the death of his wife?"

Mama nodded.

"Well, that is something from which he has never recovered. It was a deep, deep hurt to him. Oh, I know he's got to get over it—that life goes on. I know too of the tragedy you have faced. . . . But you can't measure one person with another when it comes to something that is held close in the heart."

"I know," whispered Mama.

"There are people in Chadhaven who owe a lot to Frank Cranstone—people down on their luck who have been helped by him. But you would never hear him talk about it. You see? You don't have to scratch the surface very deeply before you find that he's a kind man."

"All I can say," said Brad, "is that he hides it very well."

The kitchen door opened, and Sandor, a little sleepy-eyed, limped in wearing his pajamas.

Mama smiled and went to him. "Hullo, darling. Did we wake you? You've nothing on your feet. You're not cold, are you?"

"I was a bit hungry," said Sandor.

I gave him a sandwich, and Mama walked him toward Dr. Haisman. "This is the only one of the family you haven't met. This is Sandor."

Gravely Dr. Haisman got off the edge of the table and

put out his large hand to take Sandor's, which was already extended. Dr. Haisman matched Sandor's gravity as they greeted each other, and this put Sandor more at ease than the forced jollity with which most grownups meet children for the first time.

We ate more sandwiches and drank more coffee, and then, when Mama insisted that it was time for Sandor to go back to bed, we showed Dr. Haisman what we had done to the house. It seemed Mama had already explained our business arrangement with Mr. Slater.

"You've done wonders. I remember what this old place was like when it was empty and forlorn for so long."

Then, as he sat in his car, having said good night to all of us, he called Brad and me to him. He looked at us gravely for a few moments. "You know," he said, "Sheila Cranstone is going to need an awful lot of friendship in the days to come."

He put his car into gear and drove off.

CHAPTER THIRTEEN

AFTER DR. HAISMAN had gone, Mama, Brad, and I talked for some time about Sheila. Mama said, "It must have cost her a great deal—and it must have been a great shock to her father to see and hear his daughter come out so heavily against him in public. It's wrong that there should be trouble between a father and his daughter because of us. Sheila was wonderful—but now I am worried."

"Mama—what can we do? Mr. Cranstone looked very angry with Sheila. What will happen? Can we do anything to help her, do you think? Will he be unkind to her for what she did?"

"So many questions, Sondra. And I haven't an answer to any of them. If I thought it would help, I would go to Mr. Cranstone and plead for Sheila. But I think that would only make him more angry—and it wouldn't help Sheila. Let us wait and see, and if there comes a chance for us to help put things right between her and her father, let us be quick to take it. And one other thing, my darlings—let us never forget what she did for us."

No, I thought later, staring up at the darkness, unable to get to sleep, we'll never forget what the gentle-faced Sheila has done for us. But somehow Good Friday kept coming back to me—the day we had turned our backs on Sheila. And I thought of the sadness she had suffered in the loss of her mother, and then I wept for her.

The next morning there was another letter. It was on the mat when I was leaving to deliver papers. The address on the envelope was typewritten—but this time there was no stamp or postmark. Either during the night or in the early morning before anyone was about, the unknown writer must have delivered the letter. It was unpleasant to think that the malicious writer had actually come to our home.

This letter too was composed of words and letters cut from newspapers. It said: "Still here? Go now before it is too late."

Mama sighed. "Another visit to the police station for me."

Suddenly Brad, who had been holding the sheet of paper up to the light to see if it was the same cheap brand as before, exclaimed, "Mama—Sondra—look! See that red mark that seems to be between the stuck-on newspaper and the note paper?"

We crowded around him. There were what seemed to be two letters in red. Looking more closely, it appeared that one of the red marks might be a figure.

Brad went into the kitchen. The kettle for tea was

already on. When it began to steam, he held the letter over it and then peeled off the small piece of newspaper. The steam and heat had slightly fuzzed the writing, but there it was: "3 W," written in red ball-point pen.

My brother's face was flushed with excitement, his hands trembled. He looked at the red writing, a triumphant smile about his lips. "We've got 'em! Now we can soon find out who has been sending the letters."

"How? What do you mean, Brad?" Mama's voice was excited too.

Brad took a deep breath. "Last week—Wednesday it was—Mrs. Poplin hadn't finished numbering the papers. You know, Sondra, she pencils the number of the house —or the name—and the first or first and second letter of the road it's in on the paper to be delivered there. It's so she doesn't miss one, and it prevents Sondra and me making a mistake. Well, on Wednesday morning she overslept or something, and she hadn't finished when I arrived. So she tossed me the Wellow Road book—and I did those. I wrote the figures and the road initial with my red ball-point. That's my writing—and the newspaper from which that word 'here' was cut was delivered by me to number three Wellow Road!"

"Oh, Brad!"

Mama said, "Do you know the name of the people there?"

"It's Fenton, I think—Fenton or Lenton. I saw the name in the book, but I can't quite remember."

"After breakfast you and I will go to the police, Mr.

Detective Kopchek," said Mama, a large smile brightening her face. "Sondra can tell someone at school why you are not there. No—maybe it's better to say nothing."

Mama and Brad left immediately after breakfast, and as I had time, I stayed behind and caught up on the homework I hadn't done the night before. Sandor stayed with me until little Chunkhead Keeping called for him to go to school and then went off, limping happily along with the small friend who called him Gimpy and made it sound like a title of honor.

I scrambled through the subject I had to prepare, then stuffed my books hurriedly into my case and left the house. Walking toward our gate, I heard the front door of the Cranstones' house slam shut and feet crunch on the unseen gravel path. And then I heard Mr. Cranstone's voice, hard and cold: "And since you're so concerned about them, why not go and live with them and be one of them? That's what you seem to want. We appear to count for nothing."

Philip Cranstone's voice said, "Yes—why don't you do that? I daresay we could manage."

I saw Mr. Cranstone's car in the road by their gate and then heard the sound of bicycle wheels on the gravel. I slowed my pace, biting my lip—not because I was afraid of either of them seeing me, but because I was afraid of what I might say to them. The car door slammed, the engine started, and the car moved off. Over the hedge, I saw Phil Cranstone bob onto his cycle and ride off along the quay. Then when I walked into the road I saw Sheila wheeling her cycle slowly out of their gateway. Her face was white and strained. She saw me, and her tight lips spread into a sad smile. I went to her and kissed her, and we walked to school in silence.

Two emotions battled in me all that morning: excitement over Brad's discovery and sadness for Sheila. As the day wore on I was pleased to see that some of the tenseness left Sheila's face. But nothing was solved by that—she still had to go home that night and face again the coldness of her father and brother.

I wondered too about Dr. Haisman and Miss Slant. Something must have happened, for we didn't see Miss Slant in the school again. Much later I learned that she had accepted the suspension imposed on her by Dr. Haisman and soon afterward took a post at Minthampton.

After lunch I tried to get hold of Brad—he ought to have got to school by now, I thought. We were not supposed to encroach on the boys' side during school hours, but I saw one of the Senior boys on "neutral" ground by the administration building and asked him if he could see that a message was taken to Kopchek.

The boy, whom I didn't know, looked at me and then looked away. "Kopchek?" he said. "Never heard of him."

Then he walked away. I bit my lip. I *would* make the mistake of asking one of Philip Cranstone's cronies! I didn't see Brad after school, and Sheila and I walked home together.

"Let me push your bike for you," I said.

"It isn't any trouble."

"Well—you're walking because of me. At least let me do the donkey work of pushing it."

We smiled at each other, and Sheila surrendered the cycle to me.

"Sondra, you mustn't feel that you're to blame because of what's happened at home. Really. This has been boiling up—oh, since quite shortly after Mummy died. You see, Mummy's death was a great shock to Daddy, but he's become very bitter with everything and everybody. He's influenced Phil to be the same way. He's tried to influence me that way too. And if Debbie was old enough, he'd try to do the same with her. Your coming may be a blessing in disguise. Your being here has sort of brought Daddy to the boil. Oh, if only I could show him how wrong he's been about so many things since Mummy died."

"You don't think it's too late? That he may be too set now?"

"It may be, but I hope not. Sondra—well—I don't want you to feel badly. . . ."

This was a problem that seemed beyond me to solve—the situation between Sheila and her family.

Brad was not home from school when I went in after parting with Sheila. Mama was, though she had to go to the Hall later to lock up after a meeting of the Chadhaven Photographic Society. Sandor was gulping down his tea as fast as he could because it was his evening to go to Chunkhead Keeping's home.

The police, I learned from Mama, were delighted with Brad and questioned him closely about the writing in red ball-point pen. When they were sure he knew what he was talking about, they got a paper of the date Brad had mentioned—a daily paper published at Minthampton—and there on page two, on the other side of the front page on which Brad had written, was the word "here." It was part of a headline that read: "Foreign Warships Here."

"Leave it to us, Mrs. Kopchek," the Inspector told Mama. "We'll find whoever has been writing this nonsense in no time at all—thanks to your lad."

Mama had been only too hapy to leave it to them and had left—though Brad would have loved to stay and assist the police even further in their inquiries. He said as much, but the Inspector smiled and said that he thought the police could manage now that he had almost solved the mystery for them and that Brad had better get to school, where, the Inspector didn't doubt, more mysteries—in the way of mathematical problems—were waiting to be solved by him.

Brad came home later, cock-a-hoop over his morning success and feeling virtuous because he'd stayed on at school to catch up with what he had missed in the morning.

"And do you know, Mama," he said, "Mr. Stern actually stayed on himself to help me."

Mama said, "Like I always say—human beings are mostly nice if only they can forget to be *people* once in a while."

I'd never heard Mama voice such a sentiment before, and, in fact, I don't believe she ever had. But that was Mama—just exaggerating a little again.

The following eight or nine days are now all a jumble to me—so many things happened. Brad, who had finished painting outside, now set about putting the garden in order. We all helped in small ways. Though thinking back on the manner of our assistance, I have an idea that he would have preferred to be left on his own.

But of far more importance than this was that Sheila left home. I never knew what incident finally made her take this step, and Mama tortured herself for days about it. Sheila packed a bag one evening and moved out, cycling to her grandmother, who lived in a beautiful small house in a lane at the foot of the Quarr Hills on the outskirts of the town.

I was worried the morning I didn't see her on the way to school, but when I saw her before assembly she told me she had gone to stay with the old lady. She also said her grandmother—her father's mother—seemed to agree with what she had done.

"I'm going to have a talk with your father," the old lady had said. "Oh, don't worry, my dear, I'm not going to plead with him for you. I'm just going to give him a piece of my motherly mind. I'm surprised at him and at

Philip as well. You stay here—it will be lovely having you with me. Things have got to work themselves out."

That evening I walked up to old Mrs. Cranstone's cottage with Sheila. We had had tea, and had started to do our homework, when Mr. Cranstone arrived.

He kissed his mother, and momentarily the hard expression on his face softened. "Hullo, sweetheart," he said, "you're looking as well and as lovely as ever."

I looked up from the book in which I had buried my head when he entered the room.

Mrs. Cranstone smiled at him and patted his hand. "It's all very well, Frank," she said, "but I'm not terribly pleased with you."

He smiled wryly and said, "I didn't think you would be, Mother. But— Look, I'd like to speak to Sheila alone." His eyes took me in, and the kindness left.

I tried to rise and leave the room, but Sheila put her hand on my arm and held it firmly. "I'd like both Gran and Sondra to stay, Daddy," she said.

Mr. Cranstone looked at her and then at his mother. The old lady sat there as if she had never intended to budge an inch anyway. "Very well," he said at last. "Sheila—it's wrong for you not to be at home."

"I know it is," answered Sheila.

"Then I want you to come back with me now."

Sheila shook her head.

"I'm sorry we quarreled," her father said.

"So am I, Daddy."

"Well, then—come back home. Surely what we quarreled about isn't important?"

"So long as you believe that, I can't come home. It's very important to me."

"But . . ." Mr. Cranstone waved a hand in my direction, and I tensed myself against what he was going to say.

"Frank!" his mother exclaimed in a sharp voice. "Please—before you say anything else, I want to talk to you." She walked to the door and stood there waiting for him. Mr. Cranstone looked first at Sheila and then at me. Finally he rose, opened the door for his mother, and followed her out.

I wanted to tell Sheila that she ought to go back home, but she stopped me. "Don't let's talk about it now. Let's get on with our work."

I couldn't concentrate, and I was glad, some ten minutes later, when Mrs. Cranstone came back to the room. "Your father has gone," she told Sheila, a slight, kind smile in her eyes. "And you're staying with me." She put her hand on her granddaughter's shoulder. "Whatever happens, you must never forget that he loves you, Sheila—a very great deal. Don't do anything that's going to hurt him permanently." She picked up her sewing and sat down. "I don't know," she went on, "but it seems to me men can never stop being boys—at heart." She leaned forward and tapped first Sheila and then me on our knees with her fragile finger. "*We've* got to see that he doesn't hurt himself any more."

I was about to say that everybody seemed to be falling over themselves making excuses for him. And then I saw the old lady looking at me with a slightly raised eyebrow and again the beginnings of a smile in her eyes. "And perhaps," she said, "the brunt of it will fall on your shoulders, Sondra, my dear."

I couldn't think what Mrs. Cranstone meant, but I couldn't trust myself to speak. As I walked home, I still couldn't understand why *I* should help keep Mr. Cranstone from hurting himself.

Around this time, Philip Cranstone and some of the Senior boys became more active in their campaign against Brad. They excluded him from his favorite games—volleyball, swimming, and water polo. As the Seniors ran their games on their own, with little supervision by a master, Brad's exclusion was thought by the staff to be lack of interest on his part. He took it fairly well, though, and joined the town swimming club, which ran a water-polo team.

And then one evening Mama came home from working at the Hall and told us she had been given notice. Her job there was to end in a week's time. We found out later that Frank Cranstone had used his influence to bring this about, and it seemed that all our troubles had now resolved themselves into a feud between the Kopcheks and the Cranstones.

Although she didn't show it, I could tell that the loss of her job was worrying Mama, and when she wasn't working at the Hall during that last week, she was looking for another job.

I can't remember how may days it was after Mama and Brad had gone to the police that Dr. Haisman and the Inspector, Mr. Shute, came to tell us that the writer of the anonymous letters had been discovered. It was all part of those incident-packed eight or nine days. We were surprised to see Dr. Haisman arrive with the Inspector that evening, but delighted that he was visiting us again. It may have been my imagination, but Mama's eyes seemed brighter, her face much prettier that evening.

"Well," said the Inspector when we were all having tea in the sitting room, "the person who wrote the letters was the same one who daubed the house with mud from the marshes."

"But what had the Fentons . . . the people Brad delivered the paper to . . . against us?"

"The Fentons had nothing to do with it, Mrs. Kopchek." The Inspector looked at Dr. Haisman. "It was a boy named Arthur Stevens."

"One of Phil Cranstone's clique," said Brad as if he had suspected it all along.

"I told you the Cranstones had something to do with it." My voice was triumphant.

And then Brad said, his voice sounding deflated, "But Stevens doesn't live anywhere near Wellow Road."

The Inspector smiled—a little grimly, I thought.

Dr. Haisman said, "I think you'd better do the usual thing, Inspector, and start from the beginning."

"And we'll all keep quiet and won't burst in with questions while you are talking," said Mama, looking meaningfully at Brad and me.

The voices of Sandor and Chunkhead came to us from the castle grounds, where they were playing.

The Inspector was tall and thin, and by far the longest part of him was his legs. He crossed them, leaned over, and put his cup on the table. "The Fentons are a nice family, but poor," he said. "Mrs. Fenton is Mrs. Stevens' daily help. She goes along four mornings a week to keep the place tidy. And quite often she takes old newspapers along—to light fires or to put down when she has washed a floor and so on. It was from some of these that young Stevens cut the type to put together those ridiculous notes."

"I just *knew* Philip Cranstone had something to do with it," I said again, my voice hard and vindictive.

Dr. Haisman said, "But he didn't, Sondra. He knew nothing about it at all."

Mama looked at me. She had promised we wouldn't interrupt, and I held back the question I was on the point of asking.

The Inspector went on: "And it was young Stevens who daubed the mud over the house. The letters, the mud—he did it all entirely on his own. I'm quite satisfied from my inquiries that no one else was involved."

Mama asked, "And what will happen now?"

Inspector Shute shrugged. "He'll be brought before the Juvenile Court and charged with sending threatening letters through the post and with defacing property—insulting behavior . . ."

"Oh," said Mama, her voice soft. "Such a lot for one young pair of shoulders to carry."

"Sondra"—I looked up as Dr. Haisman spoke my name, but he was looking at Mama, who didn't seem surprised—"young Stevens is a very promising scholar. He's not good at sports, though, and because of this his position in the Cranstone clique—as Brad calls it—is a very lowly one. He wanted to show them—wanted to improve his standing among them. So he thought of this way to do it. I don't think he thought for one moment that his melodramatic letters or his stupid act in daubing the house would have any effect in making you move. He just wanted to make an impression on his friends—to build a reputation as a daredevil. He kept the cuttings of the newspaper report about the daubing of the house, and at some time or other he was going to let his friends know that he was the hero who had carried out this mysterious vendetta." Dr. Haisman smiled at Mama. "Arthur Stevens is a very frightened boy at the moment."

I thought: And it serves him right! I nearly said it aloud, but Mama sensed it and gave me a warning look.

"He is also a very intelligent boy," went on Dr.

Haisman, "and he realizes the sadness and the worry he has caused. Will you believe me, Sondra, if I tell you that he is truly contrite?"

"Of course." Mama's voice was still soft. "Must he go before the court?"

Of course he must go before the court, my mind said. He must suffer as he made us suffer.

"If he does," answered Dr. Haisman, "I believe it will spoil his chances of success in the scholarships and G.C.E. subjects for which he's studying. I don't think he can carry the strain of study and the disgrace of court proceedings as well."

"And he's only a child," murmured Mama, looking at Brad. "Can't we forget about the whole thing? The boy's suffered enough."

Dr. Haisman smiled again at Mama. "I knew you'd feel that way, my dear," he said.

Inspector Shute said, "Strictly speaking, in regard to the charge of misusing the post, the police must take action. But I think in this case justice will have been served if we take no further action." He smiled and added, "Even if a slightly blind eye has been turned to the letter of the law."

He and Dr. Haisman looked at each other briefly, and Dr. Haisman raised his eyebrows. Inspector Shute rose and said, "Excuse me," and left the room.

Within two minutes he was back again, accompanied by a boy of about fifteen—the boy who had said, "Kopchek? Never heard of him," when I had asked him to take a message to Brad. He looked pale and taut and held his hands awkwardly at his sides.

"This is Arthur Stevens, Mrs. Kopchek," said the Inspector. "I think he has something to say to you."

Mama said, "How do you do, Arthur."

The boy looked at Mama and then fixed his eyes to a spot on the carpet and began to speak, to apologize.

I didn't hear what he was saying, because my mind was full of wonder at the compassion Mama was able to show to someone who had hurt her. And while these thoughts were in my mind, I looked at Dr. Haisman and saw he was watching Mama as she listened to Arthur Stevens. It struck me then that *his* face was reflecting *my* feelings, and somehow I wasn't in the least surprised. I was only vaguely aware of Arthur Stevens leaving the room, accompanied by Brad.

Inspector Shute watched the door close after them and breathed out deeply. "Well, that's that," he said. "I think we can call it settled. I'll be off. Can I drop you, Doctor?"

Dr. Haisman looked at Mama briefly, then said, "No thank you, Mr. Shute. It's . . . er . . . a lovely evening. I think I would like to walk home."

We saw the Inspector off, then Brad came back from seeing Arthur Stevens part of the way home. We went and sat on the marsh wall. We could see Mama and Dr. Haisman as they sat talking on the settee by the French windows with the light behind them.

Brad and I looked at each other. Brad said, "Next to Father, I think Dr. Haisman is the greatest, don't you, Sondra?"

"Yes, I do," I agreed.

CHAPTER FOURTEEN

Mama finished her last week at Chad Hall and hadn't found anything to take its place. She answered advertisements and applied for jobs personally, but always, it seemed, she was just too late. Frank Cranstone was a member of the Chadhaven Chamber of Commerce, and he may have used his influence again to prevent Mama from getting a job. In the mood he was in, it was the sort of thing I believe he would have done.

And then Mr. Slater heard that Mama had lost her job, and he came around one evening, quite indignant because she had not sought his help. "I've got a vacancy for a day receptionist," he said. "My girl upped and married and left me high and dry, with the season nearly on us. And here I have been worrying myself sick over getting someone suitable in time for the big rush—and you were available all the time."

I think Mr. Slater was annoyed with himself for not thinking of Mama before and offering her the job before she lost the one she already had.

So Mama went to work for Mr. Slater. It was a more pleasant job, and she got more money for doing it. If Mr. Cranstone had been responsible for Mama's fruitless search, I thought, this was one in the eye for him.

One in the eye for him. . . . It was amazing how quickly we all picked up slang and idioms and made a point of using them whenever we could. It was all part of wanting to be accepted into our new country, and I suppose we felt they made us more English. Mama never entirely got rid of her accent, and I was pleased, for it sounded attractive. Brad, Sandor, and I, on the other hand, soon lost our accents, and we spoke English with just the suspicion of a soft, native West Country burr.

I went up to Sheila's grandmother's quite a lot. Often I would walk with Sheila from school, and we would have tea there and do our homework together.

Old Mrs. Cranstone was a dear—small, with white hair of which she was proud. It was her one vanity, and she paid regular visits to the hairdresser. Sometimes when she was reading and her face was in repose, I could see Sheila in her features—a mixture of gentleness and firmness.

At school, Miss Carson, a form mistress of about Mama's age, became deputy head, and Miss Fraser restored me to the netball team, and I played often for the school. Brad was now a regular member of the Chadhaven water-polo team. Sandor, together with untidy little Chunkhead, became a member of the Cubs and would have worn his green uniform and cap constantly had not Mama been very firm. Our life in the town was expanding. Only the cold, silent enmity of our neighbors remained. It was too close to be forgotten, and there was Sheila, an ever-present reminder that, no matter what she and her grandmother said, the family was divided because of us.

High summer was near. Long cloudless days colored everything golden. We were out in the sun as often as we could be. We did our homework on the marsh wall, and Sandor, stripped to the waist and full of the sun's life, ran and limped about.

The garden was as Brad had planned it. To the marshward side of the house, it spread in a large lawn that took in the site of the former tennis court. In the middle of it, Brad set up a bird table. On two sides—underneath the castle wall that caught the westering sun and bordering the house except where the French windows opened—the lawn was edged by flower beds. Mama had taken these over and with gay abandon had filled them with all sorts of flowers. It was perhaps a little unfortunate that she had planted most of the short, close-to-the-earth kinds first, at the back of the beds, and the taller varieties in front. It was, as Brad said, quite interesting to peer through the forest of large plants to see all the pygmies growing in the hinterland.

Mama smiled ruefully and said, "Never mind—next year I'll have them in their right places."

Brad extended the kitchen garden, which was between the house and the hedge dividing us from the Cranstones, and there he had planted cabbages, sprouts, potatoes, tomatoes, as well as some rows of runner beans. An area to the front of the house he made into a lawn, and he cleared all the rubble and rubbish from the corner of the garden at the back of the house where the trees grew.

Already "Light View" was being used as an annex to the hotel for casual visitors or tourists who required only one or two nights' accommodation—and Mama was looking happier than I had seen her since Father's death.

That was a happy summer—beautiful weather, beautiful days. Although from the end of June right through to August our house was full of visitors, it was really quite easy. All we had to do was see that beds were made and that tea was ready when our visitors were wakened. All their meals were taken at the hotel. Brad made the tea in the morning and saw that the boiler was stoked up to keep a good supply of hot water for baths. Mama and I saw to the bedmaking and the changing of bedclothes at the end of the week or when guests left. We had plenty of time to enjoy the weather. Saturday was Mama's busy day at the hotel, with old visitors leaving and new ones arriving, and we didn't see her much. Sunday was her day off, and Brad, Sandor, and I would cosset her with breakfast in bed. I would do the cooking and Brad and Sandor the fetching and carrying. But

Mama wouldn't stay in bed too long—the day always had so much to offer, and there were so many wonderful things we could do.

Sheila spent every Sunday with us, whether we went on a trip, picnicked, or just lolled around the house and garden. She said nothing about her father or Phil, but sometimes I caught her gazing at her house with a faraway look. I wondered how long this separation would last. Surely her father loved her and wanted her back.

I mentioned that to old Mrs. Cranstone one day when we were alone for a few minutes, and she said, "Of course he does, my dear. Remember I told Sheila that first evening? It's important she remembers that. But his bitterness has made him so stiff-necked that he'd rather break his own heart—and hers, bless her—before he'd make a move to put things right. And it's time he showed some sense and kindness toward your family, Sondra. What does an old sailing club matter, anyway? As for young Phil . . . But there, I suppose you can't blame him, with his father setting the example."

A few times during those months, Debbie and Sandor met on the quay, and it seemed that Debbie was about to speak but stopped herself and merely stared. And then, when Sandor smiled and said, "Hullo, Debbie," she burst into tears and fled back into her own garden and into the house. It appeared Mr. Cranstone had even succeeded in influencing little Debbie.

I think the days of most delight were those three or four Sundays we spent on Dr. Haisman's boat. He lived on the other side of the river, well beyond the boatyards, in a house with a garden that swept down smooth and green to a small creek. This small creek, which had been artificially widened to take a boat, he called Mike's Dike—his name was Michael. It led into Otter Creek, which in turn found its way to Chad Creek.

The first time Mama told us we had been invited to spend the day with Dr. Haisman on his boat was pretty awesome. We knew him as a friend who had helped us. But he was our headmaster too—an Olympian figure whose word was law. As soon as he arrived in his car to collect us all, however, I *knew* it was going to be a wonderful day.

This wasn't Dr. Haisman, respected headmaster of Chadhaven King Edward Grammar School; this was Mike Haisman, who liked to be with us and who seemed to have the effect of making Mama even happier than she already was. On the occasions he had been to our house, I had felt security, a warm glow I couldn't describe. And I'm sure Sandor and Brad felt the same.

On this Sunday, he was dressed in shorts and a short-sleeved T-shirt, and his thick forearms were browned by the sun and weather. His crew-cut prematurely gray hair took glints from the sun, and it was easy to separate this large, smiling man from the firm but kindly figure who guided hundreds of children.

Sheila came along, and we packed the car with baskets of food. We were met at Dr. Haisman's house by his widowed sister, Mrs. Passmore, who kept house for her bachelor brother. Mrs. Passmore was a large woman with a quiet voice and with a depth of character very similar to her brother's. She was maybe two or three years older than Mama and had a son at Dartmouth Naval College.

The boat, called *Spanker*, was a beauty—a white thirty-foot motor cruiser. I got these technical details, plus a lot of others I can't remember, from Brad, and we all spent the day cruising among the creeks, swimming over the side, and sun-bathing on the deck.

There was another Sunday that stands out in my memory—the day of Chunkhead's picnic. Actually it was Sandor's and Chunkhead's, but the way it turned out, it belonged to little Chunkhead.

One Sunday morning when Chunkhead was to be one of the party for the day, Mama received a deputation consisting of two small boys bursting at the seams with an idea.

Mama, Sheila, and I were in the kitchen preparing the piles of food which were necessary whenever we went out for the day.

"Mama," said Sandor. "Chunkhead and me—"

"Chunkhead and I," I corrected him as I sliced the loaf.

"Chunkhead and I have a . . . prop—"

"Purposition," prompted Chunkhead.

Sandor cast the preliminaries aside—it wasn't worth it if he were to be corrected and prompted at every turn.

"Mama—can Chunkhead and I take you all on a picnic next Sunday?"

"Of course, darling," Mama agreed, still busy with the sandwiches and without really taking in what Sandor was saying.

"A *real* picnic—with food and things, and me and Chunkhead pick the place?"

"That will be lovely," said Mama. "Now run out and play. We're busy."

Sandor took a deep, patient breath. He had experienced this sort of faraway agreement and misunderstanding of grownups before. If only they would listen properly and not think they knew all the answers before you had asked the questions.

"Mama, I mean a *real* picnic—at our secret place, and Chunkhead and me'll bring the food and drink. *You* won't have to get anything ready."

The words, this time, seeped through to Mama's busy brain. She stopped what she was doing and looked at the two eager faces looking up at her.

"My word!" she said. "And where are you going to get all this food and drink from?"

"We've saved up," answered Chunkhead proudly. "With money," he added.

"Ah, so! So you have saved up with money, eh? And you want to spend it on a picnic?"

It was obviously something which at this moment was more important to them than anything else.

Mama smiled at them. "I think it's a lovely idea. We'd all love to come."

Their relief was visible. Chunkhead said, "Everyone

will get an invisitation." The two donors of the feast looked at each other and walked importantly from the kitchen.

Mama followed them with her eyes, then smiled at Sheila and me and shrugged. "Bless their hearts," she said. "I suppose we shall learn in due course how much food *we* shall have to provide. I hope it's a fine day."

Sandor spent most of his spare time at the Keepings' now that it was vacation time. But one afternoon, he came home early and handed us all folded bits of paper, slightly finger-worn. These were the invitations. "They would have been in envelopes," he said, "but we ran out of money."

I got two, one of which I was to pass on to Sheila. The notes all read: "A picknick will be held at a secrit place on sunday all day. You are invited to attend. R.I.P. if you cannot come. Sined: S. Kopchek. G. Keeping."

Brad whispered, "Do they *mean* us to rest in peace if we can't attend?"

"Be quiet," I whispered back. "You know very well they mean R.S.V.P."

It was all very serious, and none of us smiled. Sandor said, "It will be good for you, Mama. You won't have to get any food or do anything or work or anything."

"That's wonderful, darling. But where is this secret place?"

"If I told you, it wouldn't be secret," he answered.

"But it's not far. I shall be guiding you to it. You'll be quite safe."

All day Saturday Sandor was absent. "Making arrangements," he said.

CHAPTER FIFTEEN

SUNDAY CAME, the weather was fine, and Sandor disappeared from the house early. He was back about ten o'clock, and half an hour later, he led us proudly out into the sunlight.

We walked past the castle and along the pathway bordering the marsh, which was alive with minute reed buntings piping their peeps at the sun and clinging to the reeds as they fed the livelong day. Mama was carrying a hold-all in which, I happened to know, were six large bars of chocolate—just in case something happened to go wrong with the unknown food arrangements.

For the first time I noticed how much stronger Sandor was than when we first arrived. He was tanned and wiry, and he limped ahead of us tirelessly, chattering all the time. We crossed the brook flowing into Broad Creek and continued along the path edging the Heronry until we came to Heron Creek. We pushed our way through reeds on a narrow path cutting right into the marsh by the side of the far bank of the creek.

It seemed that we were making for the sea. We could see nothing, for the reeds were more than head high, and I began to have misgivings about the site chosen for the picnic. "A secrit place . . ." Heaven help us if the place was among the reeds, on soggy ground, where the pressure of a foot brought the water up to the surface and where we were surrounded by tall reeds harboring gnats and midges and other things that bit.

But suddenly we stepped out of the reeds, and there immediately in front of us was one of the knolls which dotted the marshes here and there. It was grass covered and dry, and blackberry bushes grew there. Where the knoll jutted and sloped into the creek stood a willow tree, throwing a welcome shade, and from the gentle summit we could look to the end of the creek, where it met the open sea. Over the reeds and below us were the clear waters of the creek; the place was ideal for sun-bathing and swimming too. We had brought our swimsuits just to sun-bathe, and now we would be able to get them wet.

But what met our eyes first were Chunkhead, a fire, a small bivouac tent, a pole about five feet high to which was nailed a Union Jack, and all the signs—as Sheila said later—of this being an outpost of the Empire. What made the sight somewhat sinister to our eyes, however, was Chunkhead himself. He was stooped over the fire, on which was a billycan. From the billycan came the sound of spluttering, accompanied by a bright-blue smoke that mingled with the wood smoke from the fire and spiraled up into the gold-blue sky.

Chunkhead stooped over it, his face covered in black finger smears, with two clean channels running from the top of his face to his chin. Tears ran from his eyes as they watered from the smoke. He held a small stick in one of his black hands, and he kept prodding the concoction that slowly burned in the billycan. His spiky hair was even more spiky than usual, his tongue was fastened firmly by his lips and protruded from the corner of his mouth. His socks were down around his ankles, and his knees were covered with soot. He looked like a leprechaun brewing a cauldron of mischief with which to plague long-suffering humans.

We were on the knoll before he saw us. He looked up, and his black, streaky face displayed a big grin. He prodded the concoction in the billycan and stood up. "Hullo," he said, "I'd have had lunch ready by the time you arrived, only the sausages burst all over the place, an' I had to put on some more an' this time I remembered to dig 'em with a fork an' they're all right."

Mama beamed. "My, my, George," she said, "what a lovely spot you've found. And—and those sausages smell delicious."

"Oh, they're not the sausages," answered Chunkhead. "I've done *those*. I'm frying the potatoes now. But they're late because of the sausages. They're nearly done now, though."

I walked over and looked into the billycan. Chunkhead had slightly understated the condition of the potatoes. Not only were they done—five minutes before, they must have already been overdone. Most of them were dark brown, and some were shriveled and black. "I think they're ready now, Chunkie," I called.

"I was doing them so they'd be crisp."

Brad, who had followed me over, said softly, "Crisp! They're solid cinders."

I lifted the billycan off the fire.

"Careful," said the chef, watching anxiously. "Don't spill them!"

Sandor gave me a reproachful look for interfering and led us over to where the knoll sloped toward the water. Here a sleeping bag, a ground sheet, and a blanket were spread out. "Mama, you sit here," he said, patting the sleeping bag.

"Are we eating right away?"

Surprise took charge of Sandor's and Chunkhead's faces. "Of course. That's what Chunkhead's been doing, Mama—getting the food ready." Sandor's voice showed his disbelief that grownups could be so dense.

"Oh!" Mama sounded a little deflated. It was only eleven, and none of us were hungry. But we sat down obediently.

Brad made a tentative effort to postpone the feast by

saying to no one in particular, "I must say I prefer my sausages cold."

But it was no good. Chunkhead and Sandor were in their stride, and nothing was going to stop them. We were served with sausages and fried potatoes. The sausages were underdone, the potatoes overdone, but the pride with which we were handed our meal made us all vow to eat, no matter the cost. Mama had a china plate—which had been filched from Mrs. Keeping's dinner service. Sheila, Brad, and I were served on tin camping plates, and the two boys ate out of the billycan—one out of the lid, the other out of the frying part.

Chunkhead came around with a pile of thick slices of bread, which he put on our plates, leaving black finger marks. "You'll need that," he said, "to wipe out your plates for the afters."

"Oh, lord," Brad whispered. "Our ordeal doesn't end with *one* course."

The afters were tinned peaches, which Chunkhead flopped out directly from the tin onto our bread-wiped plates. It was probably a good thing Mama had not seen the operation which resulted in the opening of the tin. We waited for spoons.

"No spoons," said Chunkhead happily. "We forgot 'em, didn't we, Gimpy? Never mind. You can eat 'em with your fingers—like this." He showed us.

"And drink the juice like this," said Sandor, tilting the billycan lid to his mouth and pouring the juice down his throat and chin onto his T-shirt.

Mama said, "Of course, that's how it's done when you're out in the wilds." She followed their example with gusto.

"Mama," I protested, "you needn't be *quite* so enthusiastic."

Mama drained the juice from her plate and smacked her lips as some of the juice trickled down her chin.

"You're too fussy, Sondra, sweetheart. Out in the wilds we eat like this all the time," she said.

Sheila was making an effort to drink her juice from the plate, Brad had already done so, and I, after managing to pick up the slippery slices of fruit in my fingers, followed suit.

It was only when we had finished that we remembered we could have used our forks.

The washing up was done by Sandor—in cold water—and he refused all offers of help, wiping the utensils dry with newspaper.

"Ah, well," said Brad philosophically as he watched the operation with horror-struck fascination, "they say you have to eat a peck of dirt before you die."

They made us syrup-sweet tea, the color of teak, with minute particles of wood ash floating in it. They stood, happily anticipating our delight.

Later we changed into our swimsuits and sun-bathed for a while. The air was still but for the faint buzzing of insects, the cheeps of the buntings, and the occasional plop of a fish in the creek.

Suddenly the afternoon tranquillity was shattered by

a shrill shout from Sandor. The cry sent a thick flutter of buntings up from the reeds like dust beaten from a carpet and caused Sheila to squeak in dismay. Brad sat up with a start, and Mama was awakened from a doze in one violent movement. "Someone's run over a dog!" she called.

But Sandor had merely sighted a sailing craft bearing up the creek from the sea. "Shin up to the crow's-nest, Chunkhead," he said, "and spy out who the invaders are."

The crow's-nest proved to be the top of the dumpy, pollarded willow tree, up which Chunkhead shinned as directed. As the crow's-nest was no higher than the summit of the knoll—since its base was near the water—it wasn't clear to us exactly what advantages Chunkhead's exertions brought. But doubtless Sandor and Chunkhead knew.

"It's Vikings from Chadhaven," cried Chunkhead hoarsely, shading his eyes with his hand and gazing dramatically toward the boat.

"We've beaten them before, we shall beat them again!" Sandor said heroically, and limped to a blackberry bush, from the depths of which he produced two models of repeating rifles. He ran back to the tree and handed one of them to Chunkhead. Then he flung himself full-length on the ground behind the tree and leveled his weapon at the boat.

"Vikings and rifles?" said Brad, viewing the dramatic developments with a calm interest.

Sandor looked pityingly over his shoulder, withering Brad with his expression. "Of course," he said. "These are modern Vikings. You take care of the women and children while we fight them off."

He turned to the business in hand, adding his fire power to that of Chunkhead's, who was already "peeowing" shot after shot at the boat. "Peeow!" went Sandor, pulling his trigger. But even with shot raking it from stem to stern, the invaders' boat moved doggedly on.

"Aim for the water line," yelled Chunkhead.

"Peeow!" went Sandor.

The disclosure of the armory in the blackberry bush stirred Mama, for she was looking with an added interest at the camp site—the tent, the cooking utensils, the flag on the pole, the blanket, the sleeping bag, and the ground sheet—and I saw one of her eyebrows rise, a sign that Mama had solved some problem or other that had been puzzling her.

The craft was now quite close, and our stout defenders were "peeowing" themselves into a frenzy. Suddenly Sheila rose, looking intently at the boat. I followed her gaze and stood up too. In the craft were Mr. Cranstone, Phil, and Debbie.

"Hold your fire!" Sandor ordered.

"What for?" said Chunkhead, disgust in his voice.

"They're friends," said Sandor, scrambling to his feet. He waved. "Hi, Debbie!" he shouted.

Debbie waved excitedly. Frank Cranstone looked toward us, and Phil, at the tiller, turned his head. They spoke briefly together, then the boat turned and began tacking toward the mouth of the creek.

Sheila's hand was half raised to wave, but the coldness of her father's action discouraged her.

Mama noticed. "Come on, Sheila, sweetheart," she said. "Help me make a cup of tea."

"I thought you said it was a friendly craft," said Chunkhead.

"Well, we'll pretend Debbie isn't there," said Sandor. "Come on! We've got 'em on the run. Let's send 'em on their way."

"Peeow!" went Chunkhead happily.

"Peeow!" agreed Sandor.

With the enemy beaten off, Sandor said, "All right, Chunkhead, we've done it again. You can come down now."

With the air of a conqueror, Chunkhead turned to climb down. His foot slipped, and suddenly he was suspended above the water from an overhanging branch by the seat of his trunks.

A look of astonishment took charge of his face, and we could not help but laugh.

Chunkhead eyed us reproachfully. "I shall get wet," he said.

Laughing still, Brad waded into the creek until he was standing under Chunkhead, suspended some two feet above him.

"All right, Chunkie," said Brad. "Wriggle yourself free. I'll catch you."

"You laughed," said Chunkhead, condemnation in his voice. "How do I know you won't drop me in the drink?"

"I promise."

"Huh." Chunkhead gave the impression of not being entirely convinced.

"All right. Wriggle free on your own—and you're bound to drop in the drink anyway."

"All right," Chunkhead said as if bestowing a favor. "Here I come, then." He jerked and kicked and moved his arms about like someone swimming through the air, while Brad braced himself. Finally there was a snap and Chunkhead dropped. Brad staggered, but managed to stay upright. He unhitched the small piece of branch still adhering to Chunkhead's seat and then waded ashore with him.

Chunkhead scrambled free of his undignified position as soon as he saw dry ground. He looked at us all reproachfully again. "I might have got wet," he said.

"Coo," said Sandor, understanding how his friend felt. "That was a narrow squeak, Chunkhead."

But now Chunkhead, who knew only too well how narrow had been his escape, was too full for words.

Mama's tea went down well. We bathed and sunbathed again, and then it was time to make for home.

Neither of the boys made any attempt to pack up their kit, and Mama said, "How did you two manage to get all this stuff here?"

"We brought it bit by bit," said Sandor.

"And left it here? Not afraid of it being stolen?"

"It's a secrit place," said Chunkhead.

"Oh, well," said Mama. "Now, are we all ready to go? We'll help you pack."

"Well . . . er . . ."

And then, under Mama's probing questions, it all came out. Chunkhead's parents were under the impression that he was some seventy miles away, camping with the Wolf Cubs. He was supposed to have been away for the past week—and for the following week too. But because Sandor hadn't been allowed to go, Chunkhead had not wanted to go without his friend. It had been his idea to stay behind and take all his camping equipment to the knoll in the marshes so that, except at night, Sandor could enjoy all the delights of camping life.

At night, Chunkhead had been content to stay out alone on the lonely, whispering marshes so that he could be with his friend during the day. He had kept the money given to him for the Cub camp to feed them both. Sandor had done the shopping in the town, while Chunkhead stayed in the marshes for fear he might run into his mother or father. He didn't want to go to the Cubs' camp if Sandor couldn't go.

Mama hugged the grubby little form of Chunkhead to her. "You're a darling boy, George," she told him. "And we all love you for what you've done for Sandor."

Mama fixed everything with Mr. and Mrs. Keeping, and Brad went out each night of the following week to bivouac with two of the happiest boys in Chadhaven.

For Mama let Sandor camp out after this demonstration of friendship.

George (Chunkhead) Keeping, all four feet two inches of him, had crept into our hearts—grubby face, mud-covered knees, concertina socks, and all.

CHAPTER SIXTEEN

SUMMER PASSED all too quickly. Old Mrs. Cranstone and Sheila went away for three weeks during August. All through July and August "Light View" was in full use as the hotel annex, and Mama was kept hard at work but happy at the hotel. Brad and I continued with our paper route in the early mornings and lazed the days away, soaking up the sun. Mr. Keeping had a dinghy which he lent us, and with Sandor and Chunkhead we explored the creeks and marshes. We did our school-vacation tasks and read in the sun.

The weather broke during the last week in August, and the sun-parched land was drenched with rain that fell for days. The Chad, fed by the water draining from the hills, rose almost frighteningly and rushed through the town, riotous and red with the mud the streams brought from the hills. September came, soggy and gray, and by the time we returned to school, people were saying it was the wettest period in the district for thirty years.

Still there was no sign of a break in the ice that encased Frank Cranstone, no sign of a healing of the breach between him and Sheila.

I suggested that she should make the first move—go to her father and tell him she would have nothing more to do with us. It wasn't right that a family should be split because of outsiders.

Sheila shook her head. "I can't do that, Sondra. You can't turn friendship off and on, or destroy a friendship, just like that. If I went back now, Daddy would tell himself that he'd won—that he'd proved to me and to himself that his attitude of bitterness is right. And we would go on as before. He would find something else to vent his bitterness on. Don't you see? I told you before that your coming to Chadhaven and 'Light View' just brought things to the boil. My going back now will solve nothing—and I should hate myself for the rest of my life for being weak and not admitting that you are my friends."

So we went on as before, Sheila dividing her time between her grandmother and us. And it seemed to me, on the few occasions I saw Mr. Cranstone and we passed silent and cold, that, knowing how much time his daughter spent with us, his face grew harder and harder.

The thought of Sheila nagged at Mama, spoiling her happiness. For now she had a number of friends in the town, Dr. Haisman visited us more often, and she liked her work. Also, Brad and I were doing well at school, and Sandor was growing as strong as a young ox.

"Maybe," Mama said, "it's selfish of me to feel this way. Everything else is so wonderful. But I can't feel completely happy while there is this thing between the Cranstones and us and between Sheila and her father. Just this—and it spoils everything else for us. That's selfish, I know. But if only there was something . . ."

The more we thought, however, the more it seemed there was nothing anyone could do. There was just no approaching Frank Cranstone, and I had the feeling that as far as we Kopcheks were concerned, he was only waiting—waiting for the slightest chance to pounce and destroy our new-found happiness.

And then came that Friday evening near the end of September. The wind had blustered and it had rained for most of the day. But just before we finished afternoon school, the rain stopped, and the gusting wind eased its battering. Occasional breaks appeared in the clouds, and, beyond them, bits of blue sky could be seen. Once or twice the sun managed to show itself from the west, and the drenched, gray countryside was fleetingly touched with watery gold.

Brad and I had gone with Sheila to her grandmother's straight from school. We had had tea and had done some of our homework before we set off for home. The wind still gusted occasionally and the Chad roared. We put our heads down and walked along Fore Street toward the quay.

It was dusk by the time we reached the end of Fore

Street to turn onto the quay, and it was then that tragedy came and stood close to us for what seemed an eternity.

We were crossing the green when we heard a shout, followed by Debbie's voice. A moment later the small figure of Debbie shot out of the Cranstones' gateway shouting, "No! No! I want Sheila and Sandor!"

She ran on blindly across the narrow strip of road between the houses and the edge of the quay. She turned her head to see where she was going only when she was less than a yard from the edge.

Stupidly I screamed, "Debbie!"

But she couldn't stop herself, and we saw her disappear over the edge into the red, swirling waters of the Chad. At the same time, two figures appeared at the gates of the two houses. One was Mr. Cranstone, who had arrived at the gate as Debbie fell. The shock of it seemed to rob him of the power of movement. The other was Sandor, who rushed out of the gateway of "Light View" in his limping run shouting, "Debbie! Debbie!"

He didn't hesitate, but jumped off the quayside into the river.

I was aware of Brad running in front of me and tearing off his macintosh and of my legs, which felt trembly and useless, carrying me after him. And then I felt the chill of the water clutch me and surround me. I pushed my way to the surface, feeling myself being carried seaward. I saw Brad, farther out in midstream, take a deep breath and dive.

Behind me I was vaguely aware of another splash as I struck out for the spot where I had seen Brad dive. He broke surface some twenty yards downstream from where I saw him force himself under. He had one of them. I looked frantically about me for a sign of the other, but in the twilight it was difficult to see much. I swam to Brad, who was unable to make any headway against the flow. I reached him and together we began moving across the current toward the reeds.

The limp figure we held between us was Debbie. There was no sign of Sandor, and, swimming and helping Brad keep Debbie's head above water, I wept, my sobs choking me.

Dimly I could see Brad's face, strained with effort, drawn and stricken also with the realization of what had happened.

We were among the reeds now. We could stand, sinking in the ooze until the water came above our waists. Brad lifted Debbie and stood breathing harshly and deeply. The river had overflowed, and we began wading through the reeds toward the shale foreshore below the wall of our house.

Sandor's name kept throbbing in my head. We squelched onto the shale where Mama stood. She took Debbie from Brad, laid her face down on the wet foreshore, and squeezed her lungs free of water. Mama's face was like Brad's as she worked. She said nothing. I went into the house for a blanket. I didn't know if Debbie was alive. When I came out again, Mama was standing with Debbie in her arms, and Brad was gone. We wrapped the blanket around the little girl and began walking toward the slope at the end of the quay leading to the road.

Suddenly there came a sound behind us—the movement of feet splashing through water. We turned to see Brad staggering with Sandor in his arms, followed by Mr. Cranstone, in dripping shirt and trousers. And I remembered now the splash I had heard behind me in the river and knew it had been Mr. Cranstone.

Brad was weak and trembling with cold, and I took the frightened Sandor from his arms. Mr. Cranstone came toward us, and Mama handed him the blanketed Debbie.

"Thank you," he said, breathing unevenly.

"And thank you for going after Sandor," replied Mama.

Mr. Cranstone came into our house, and Mama tended to both children until the doctor arrived. And once the doctor had pronounced them both only a little the worse for what had happened, Mama carried Debbie to the Cranstones' house and put her to bed.

The following morning before breakfast there was a knock on the door. I went to answer, but Mama was there before me. Framed in the doorway was Frank Cranstone, and he had Debbie in his arms.

Mama smiled, "Come in, Mr. Cranstone. Hullo, Debbie, sweetheart." She led the way into the dining room, where Brad had already lighted the fire before going out on the paper route.

Mr. Cranstone said, "I have to go into Minthampton this morning, and Debbie must stay in bed today."

Debbie, still in nightie and dressing gown and wrapped in a pink blanket, shook her head.

Mama said, "It's what the doctor ordered, sweetheart."

"She wants to be with Sandor."

"I'm *glad* you brought her. We're just going to have a cup of tea. Perhaps . . ."

"I've just had breakfast, but—I think I'd like one."

I went out to the kitchen to get the tea. When I returned, Mama and our neighbor were seated in chairs on either side of the fireplace, and Mama had Debbie on her lap.

Mr. Cranstone was saying, "And when I told her to stop talking through the hedge to Sandor or I'd send her away, she ran out of the gate . . ."

"And into the river, and plop went Sandor after her." Mama could even smile about it now.

The bitterness had gone from the lean face of Mr. Cranstone, and now there seemed almost a shyness and anxiety about him. He said, "*You* know what I should be saying to you, Mrs. Kopchek."

"And I should be saying something similar to you," said Mama. "But I think maybe what has happened has done away with the need to say it."

Mr. Cranstone sipped his tea. After a few moments he

said, "On my way to Minthampton I'm calling at my mother's. I hope Sheila will make the trip with me."

"She will," said Mama. "And she'll be very happy."

He smiled ruefully. "It isn't until some of us have the things we cherish more than anything nearly snatched from us that we come to our senses. I wonder why we make it so difficult for ourselves?"

"We don't value things as we should if we come by them easily," Mama said. "People say that all the time, but it's funny—we're always surprised when the truth of it is shown."

Mr. Cranstone stood up and put his empty cup on the table. He kissed Debbie good-by. I took her from Mama, and Mama went with him to the door. On the step he turned and said, "There have been very few things more wonderful in my life than the sight of young Sandor jumping into that river to save Debbie. We'll try to *deserve* to be living next door to somebody like that."

Easter is here again. Have we been in England and Chadhaven only just over a year? Over in the castle ruins I can hear the voices of Sandor and Chunkhead. It seems they're rescuing Debbie from the fiery dragon. They're making enough noise for the dragon too. Brad and Phil Cranstone are tinkering with the outboard engine of the dinghy. It's in pieces all over our lawn, and if they ever get it together again it'll be a miracle. And even if they do, I'll bet they have a part left over and won't know where in the world it came from.

I have just finished making the beds for the five visitors we have from the hotel for the Easter holidays. I've just heard Mama talking to Mr. Cranstone, fixing the time we shall be ready on Bank Holiday morning, for we're all spending the day on Dr. Haisman's boat, and we're going over in Mr. Cranstone's car. There will be nine of us including Chunkhead, so it looks as if Mr. Cranstone will have to make two journeys. Unless Sheila and I cycle over. We could do that. Oh, I *do* hope this lovely weather holds out. We have had a hard winter, and we all need the sun.

If Sheila doesn't hurry up, I'm going across to make her hustle. . . . Everything looks so wonderful from my window. There's a slight haze out to sea beyond the marsh, and from where I am I can't see a cloud anywhere. Those children over in the castle! What a row they're making! And Debbie's nearly as bad as the two boys. Mama is singing in the kitchen. Maybe you can measure happiness by noise sometimes. Oh, Brad's pinched his finger with the pliers or something, and now *he's* making a noise. But you couldn't measure *his* happiness by the noise he's making! And Phil is laughing his head off.

Until Sheila comes, I'll go down and see if I can help Mama in the kitchen. . . . Mama . . . bless her, she's put roots down for us in happy soil—and there *was* a time when I said and felt I hated the place. And now I never want to leave Chadhaven and the friends we have here.

Perhaps that's what made it so difficult—for me, anyway—when we first came here. I had never known in the old country what being friends really meant—I never had one. Until Sheila—there she is now. I can hear her calling.

Great heavens! Here I am dreaming up here, looking out of my window—and I haven't done my hair. I'll do it downstairs, and then Sheila and I can both give Mama a hand in the kitchen before we go into the town to do the shopping.

Oh, it's a wonderful day! And the forecast is fine for tomorrow—and tomorrow and the day after tomorrow. . . .